Over My Head

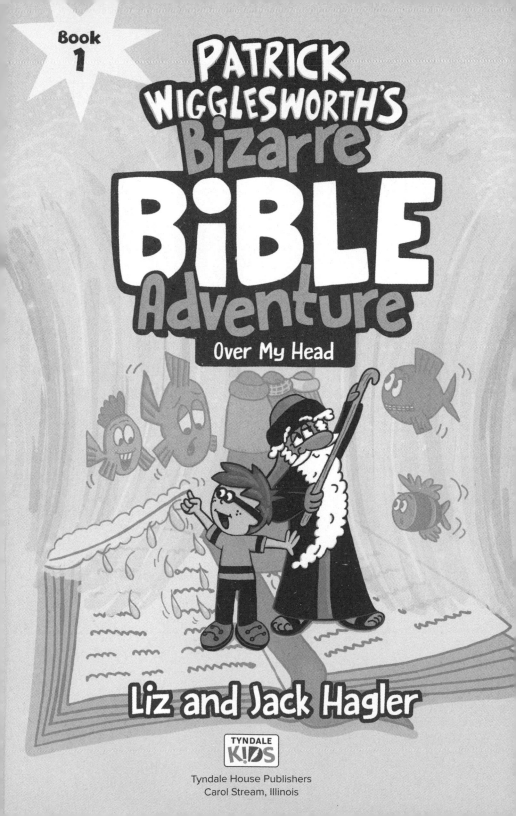

Book 1

PATRICK WIGGLESWORTH'S Bizarre BIBLE Adventure

Over My Head

Liz and Jack Hagler

TYNDALE KIDS

Tyndale House Publishers
Carol Stream, Illinois

Visit Tyndale's website for kids at tyndale.com/kids.

Visit the authors' website at patrickwigglesworth.com.

Tyndale is a registered trademark of Tyndale House Ministries. The Tyndale Kids logo is a trademark of Tyndale House Ministries.

Over My Head

Designed by Eva M. Winters

Edited by Deborah King

Published in association with the literary agency of Brentwood Studios, 1550 McEwen, Suite 300 PND 17, Franklin, TN 37067.

This book is a work of fiction. Where real people, events, establishments, organizations, or locales appear, they are used fictitiously. All other elements of the novel are drawn from the authors' imagination.

For manufacturing information regarding this product, please call 1-855-277-9400.

For information about special discounts for bulk purchases, please contact Tyndale House Publishers at csresponse@tyndale.com, or call 1-855-277-9400.

Library of Congress Cataloging-in-Publication Data

A catalog record for this book is available from the Library of Congress.

ISBN 978-1-4964-6296-1

Printed in the United States of America

29	28	27	26	25	24	23
7	6	5	4	3	2	1

To Alistair, Gilbert, and Levi.
Love, Mimi and Papa Jack.

DISCLAIMER!

THIS JOURNAL TELLS
THE STORY OF
WHAT I SAW ON
MY BIBLE ADVENTURE.
IT MIGHT SEEM
A LITTLE DIFFERENT
FROM WHAT YOU READ
IN YOUR BIBLE.
BUT DON'T WORRY—I'VE
INCLUDED BIBLE VERSES
SO YOU CAN LOOK UP
EACH STORY.

THANKS,
PATRICK

THURSDAY...

Who names their kid PATRICK PADDY
Wigglesworth?

Mom says she loves the name Patrick
because it means...

NOBLEMAN

I don't care what it MEANS, because at
MY school the name Patrick makes you
a PINCH TARGET every St. Patrick's Day.

PINCH
MARKS

STOP
I'M
WEARING
GREEN!

MORE
PINCH
MARKS

As for my middle name, Mom HAD to let Dad pick that one. Here's why!

OVER 80'S STATE BOWLING CHAMPIONSHIP!

ME

HEY, UNCLE PADDY, ONE MORE STRIKE AND WE'LL NAME OUR BABY AFTER YOU!

OK, WATCH THIS!

Anyway...my weird name is not the FREAKIEST part of my story. Ever since the day I was born in Gasket, California, my life has just gotten weirder and weirder.

Day 1: When I was only 6 hours old, Horace Gasket Hospital LOST me.

HORACE GASKET HOSPITAL
——— ON MY BIRTH DAY ———

WE LOST A BABY!

OH, NO!

HELP!

← BROOM CLOSET

Age 1: I got locked in my car seat. It took the JAWS OF LIFE to get me out.

Age 2: Mom posted my potty training success on the Internet, and it went VIRAL!

Age 3: My little sister, Marlee, was born TALKING.

Age 4: I found my Grandma McAllister's dentures in my burger.

Age 5: My baby lizard grew up to be an ALLIGATOR.

FYI...Dad made me get rid of TINY when he got too big to sleep in the bathtub.

Age 6: While camping, I sleepwalked into an animal trap.

Age 7: My parakeet, Pete, ate my homework.

Dad said, "Goodbye, paper-eating Pete."

Age 8: I caught a fly ball with my teeth.

Age 9: My best friend, Billy Zwingli, and I nearly drowned in a puddle that should have had its own lifeguard.

So it's no surprise that at age 10, another CRAZY FREAKY WEIRD THING happened...

...I got YANKED into a Bible adventure!

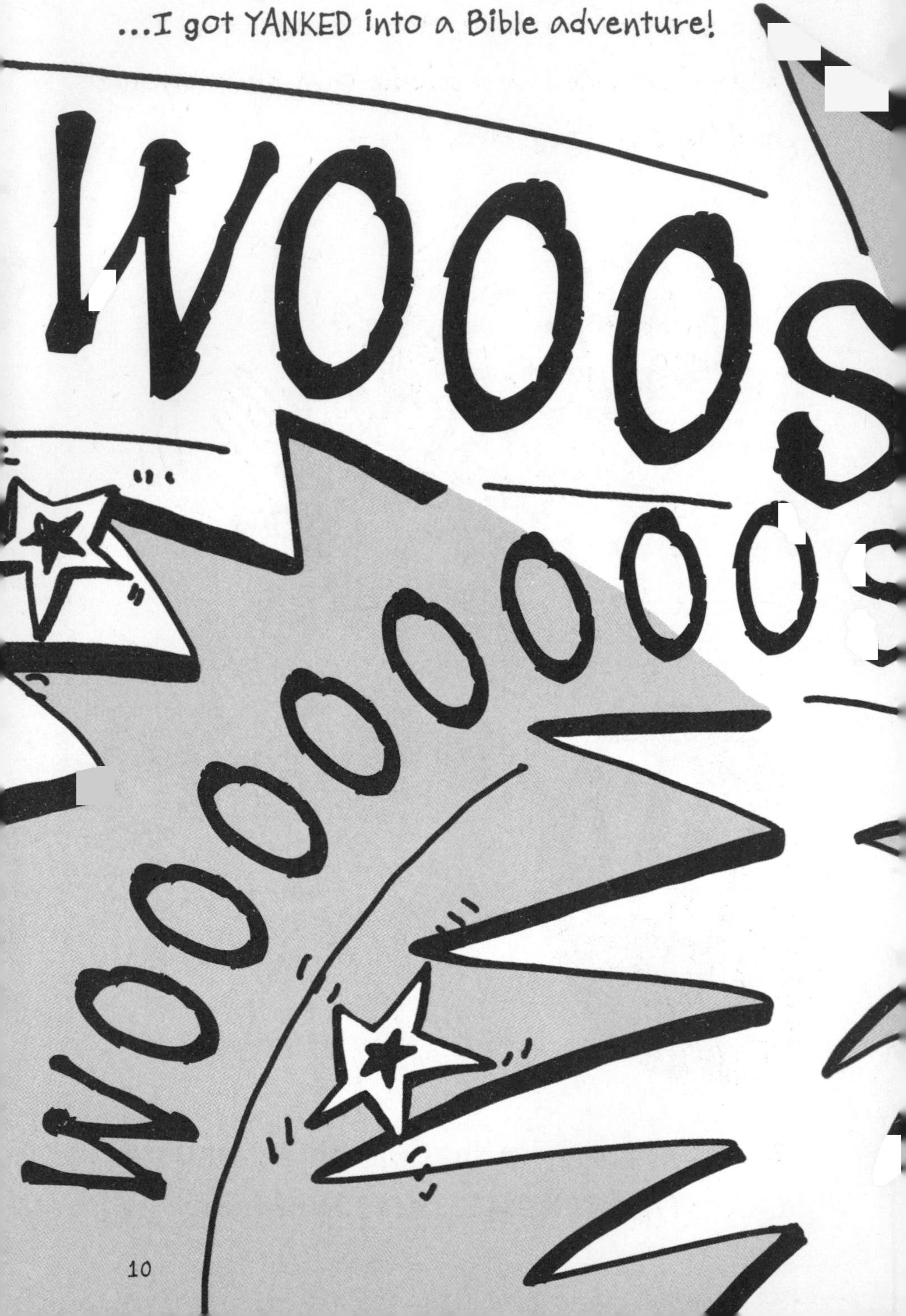
WOOOS
WOOOOOOOOOOS

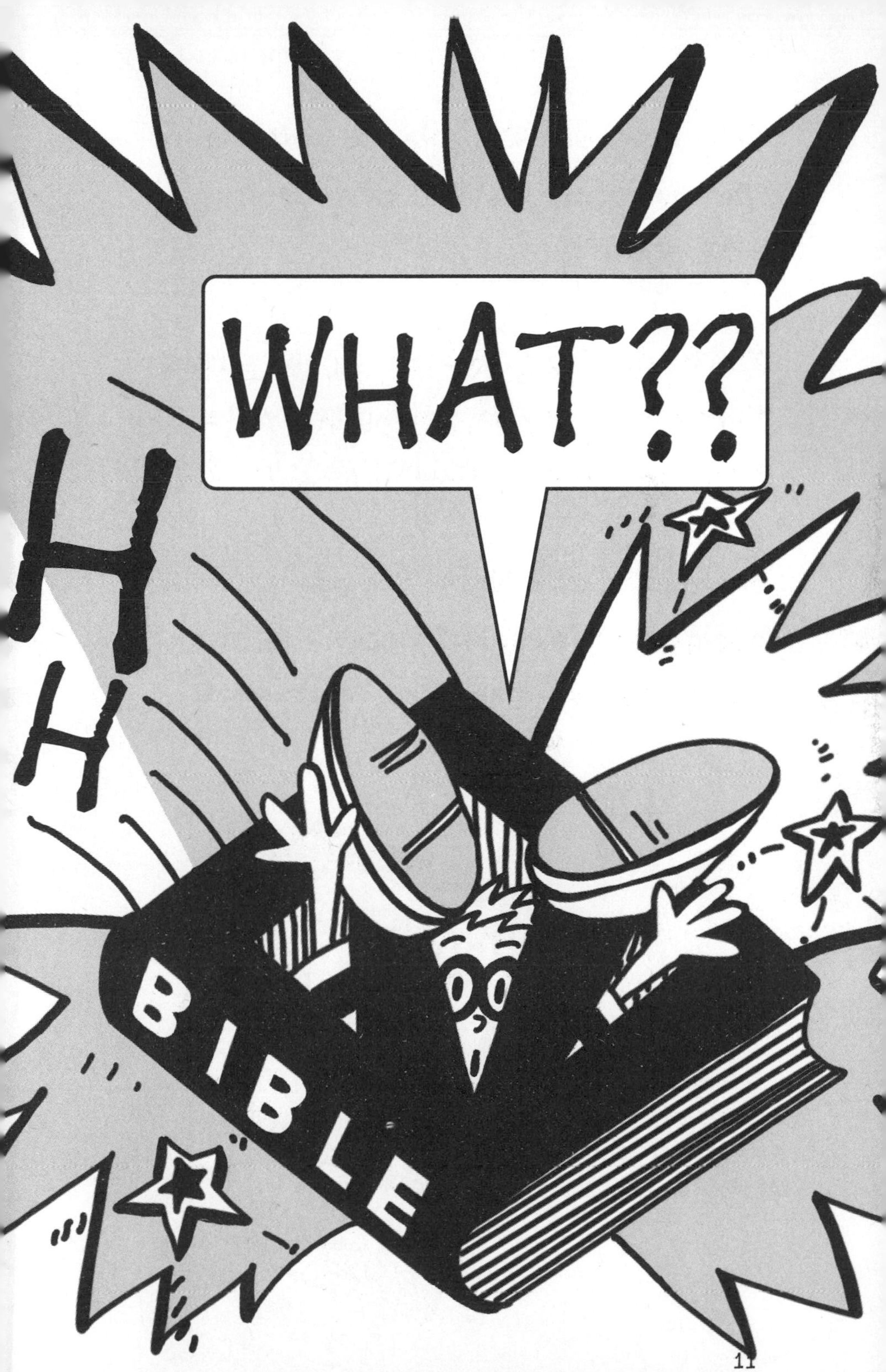
WHAT??
H
H
BIBLE

And of course, I'm going to write down what happened on MY Bible adventure. Who wouldn't?

I'm also going to record ALL the strange things that keep happening in my life. I'm sure my readers wouldn't want to MISS OUT.

Thankfully, with all the 4th grade writing assignments Mrs. McPherson has given us this fall, I've had lots of practice.

Here's a sample of one of my essays...

I'll swap my cat for your Dog!

By Patrick W.

and one of my cartoon drawings.

After all, you never know when a Bible adventure journal might come in handy.

SATURDAY...

But let's back up a bit. It all began one week
ago on a regular rainy, NOTHING TO DO...

Saturday morning in Gasket, California. My
friend Billy was busy, which left me lying
alone on my bed staring...

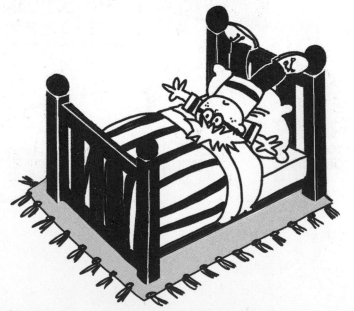

...at a spider rappelling down the wall,

...at my Spider-Man comic book collection on my bookshelf,

...and at my Bible sitting next to my Spider-Man comic collection.

Well, you know how one thing can lead to another. Staring at my Bible led to picking up my Bible...

which led to opening my Bible...

which led to actually reading my Bible...

which led to blurting out a bunch of questions...

1. WHY IS THIS BOOK SO THICK AND CONFUSING?

2. WHAT DOES IT HAVE TO DO WITH MY LIFE?

3. WHERE ARE THE CARTOONS?

What do you know—SOMEONE WAS LISTENING! Because that's when I got yanked into my Bible adventure.

PITCH
BLACK
EVERYW

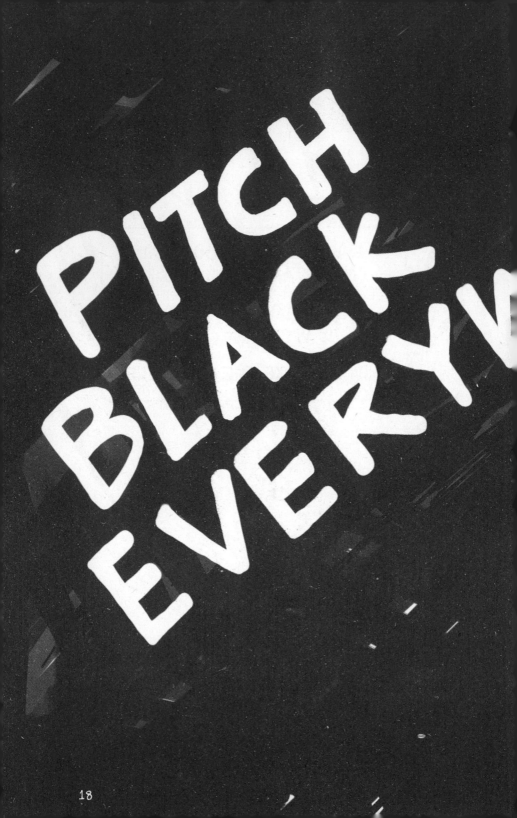

WHERE

I MEAN EVERYWHERE!

Was I scared?

PETRIFIED!!!

Till a deep voice spoke.

NOW WHERE IS THAT OIL LAMP?
I KNOW I'M SUPPOSED TO TAKE
PATRICK THROUGH THE FIRST FIVE
BOOKS OF THE BIBLE, BUT HOW
CAN I READ MY TOUR NOTES IN
THE DARK? AH, HERE IT IS.

Suddenly a lamp illuminated a man

reading a book.

OK, I GOT IT.
PATRICK NEEDS
A FRIENDLY
GREETING.

I remembered enough from Sunday school to know who wrote the first 5 books of the Bible, so I put 2 and 2 together. This must be Moses.

Moses' lamp got me thinking. Maybe I had a flashlight in my pocket so I could help him out. But unfortunately, even though I DID find my Spider-Man flashlight in my right pants pocket, the BATTERIES

WOULDN'T WORK.

As it turned out, I really never needed my flashlight, for right after Moses' welcome speech, the light came on.

DAY 1 - GOD MADE LIGHT!

You know how you get a BRAIN FREEZE when you eat ice cream too fast? Well, I got EYE FREEZE from the light!

Luckily, squeezing my eyes tight for 10 seconds unfroze them, because when I reopened them...I found myself not only visiting DAY 1 of Creation, but ALL 7 DAYS!

And Moses wasn't kidding. Next I had to leap out of the way of a giant mountain bursting through an ocean.

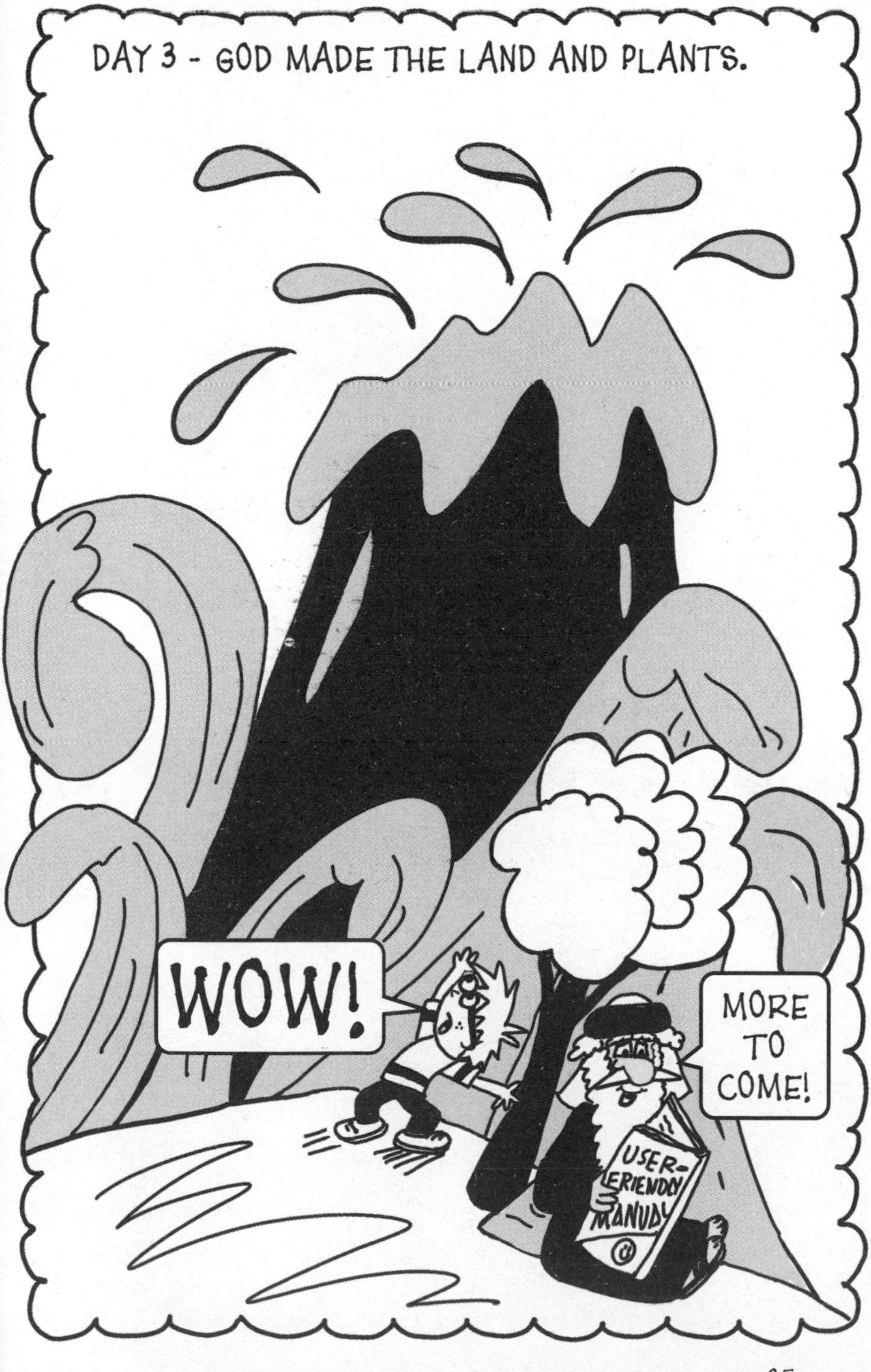
DAY 3 - GOD MADE THE LAND AND PLANTS.
WOW!
MORE TO COME!
USER-FRIENDLY MANUAL

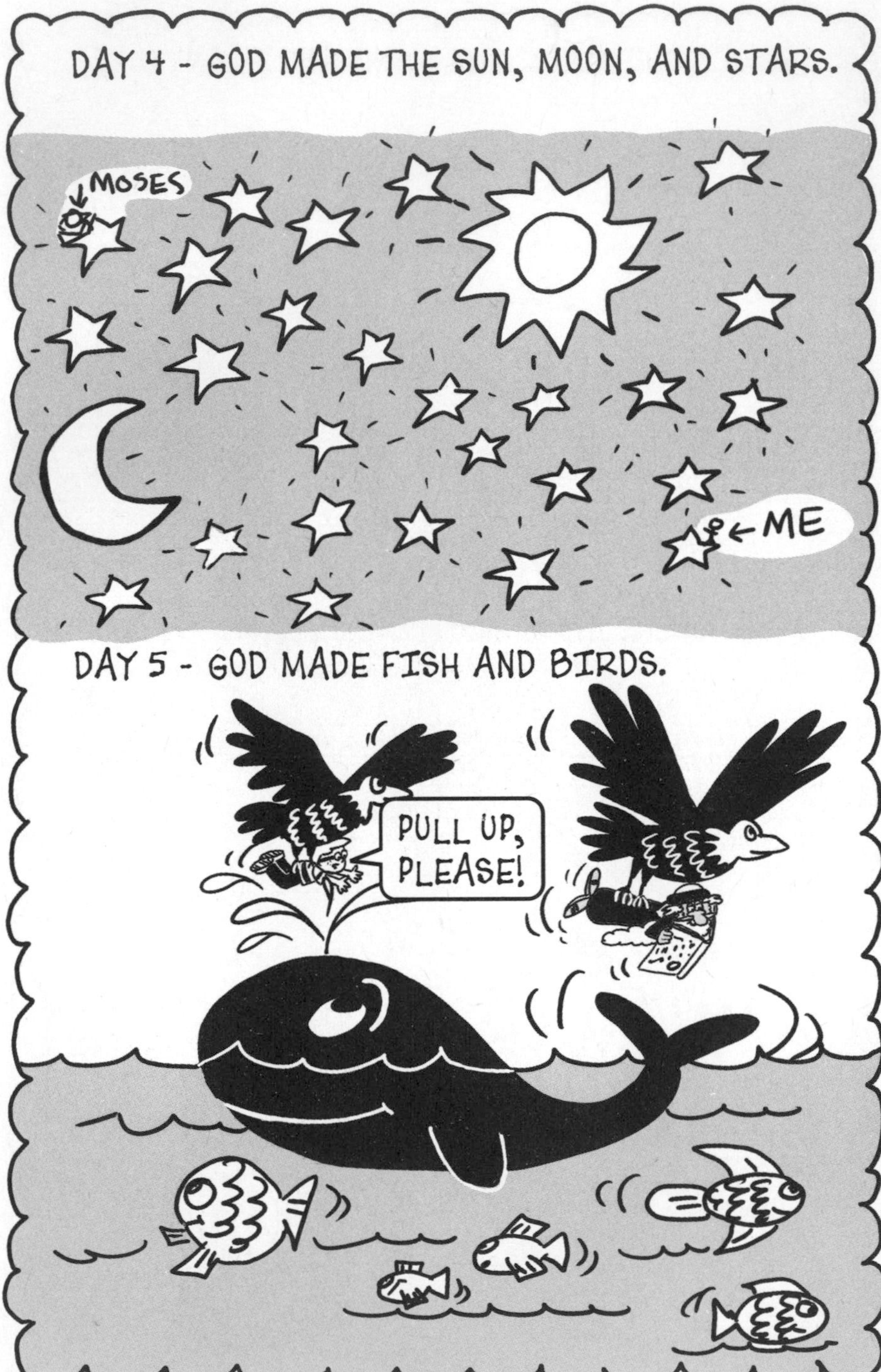
DAY 4 - GOD MADE THE SUN, MOON, AND STARS.
MOSES
ME
DAY 5 - GOD MADE FISH AND BIRDS.
PULL UP, PLEASE!

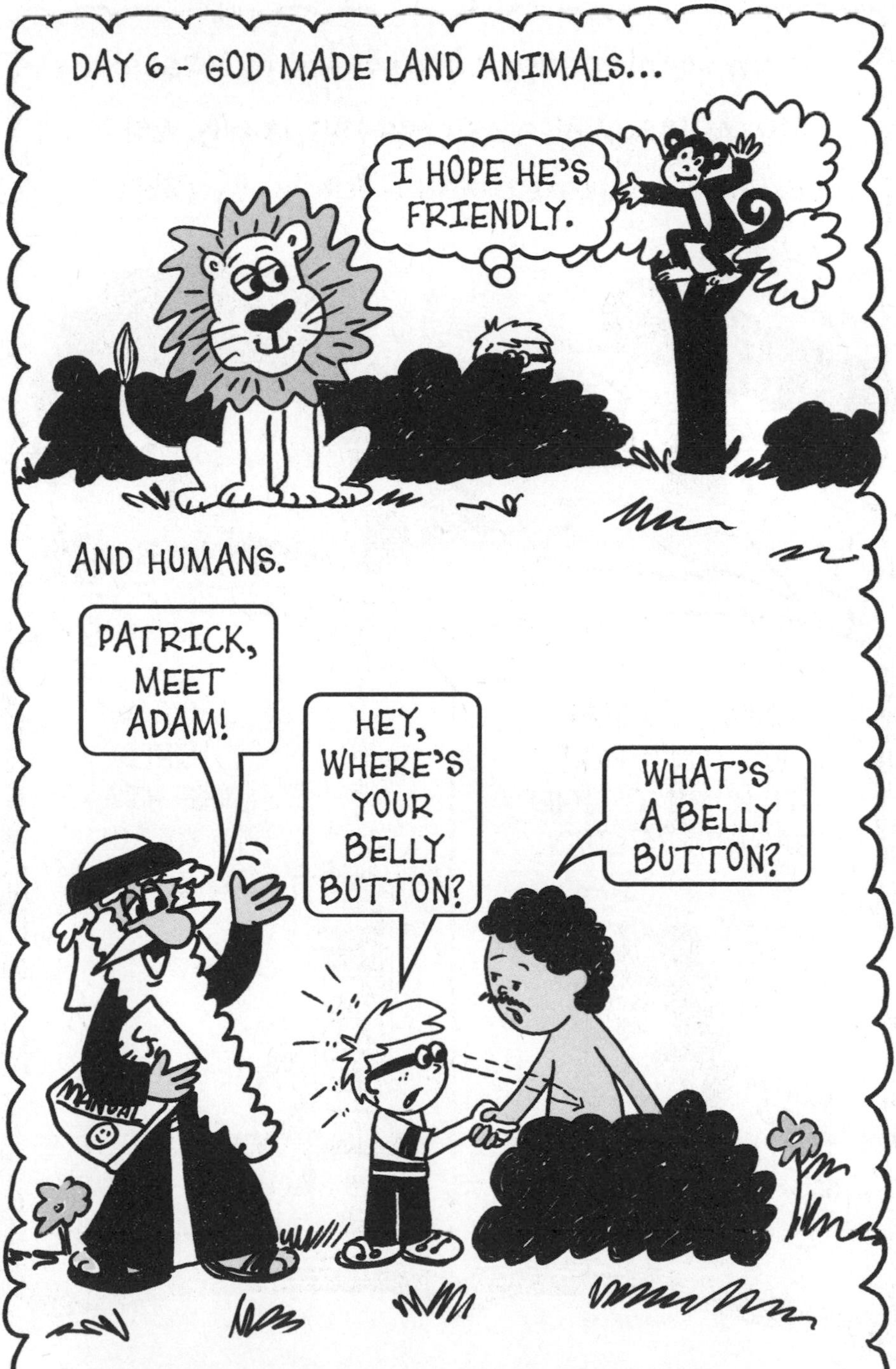
DAY 6 - GOD MADE LAND ANIMALS...
I HOPE HE'S FRIENDLY.
AND HUMANS.
PATRICK, MEET ADAM!
HEY, WHERE'S YOUR BELLY BUTTON?
WHAT'S A BELLY BUTTON?
MANUAL

Adam seemed super interested in Moses' tour notes, which worked out really well because Adam also had a job in my Bible adventure.

ADAM, TO MAKE PATRICK FEEL AT HOME IN THE GARDEN OF EDEN,

PLEASE USE LABELS LIKE HIS 4TH GRADE TEACHER.

Then Moses showed Adam the secret compartment in the back of the book with supplies.

THE TOUR NOTES CALL IT A SHARPIE.

And Adam knew exactly what to do.

PATRICK, IT'S TIME FOR ME TO NAME ALL OF GOD'S CREATURES.

OH FUN, LABELS! I WANT TO HELP OUT!

Just when I needed it, I found some tape in my right pants pocket. Seemed like this was part of my Bible adventure. Unfortunately the tape didn't stick on EVERYTHING.

THE BIRD LABELS BLEW OFF.

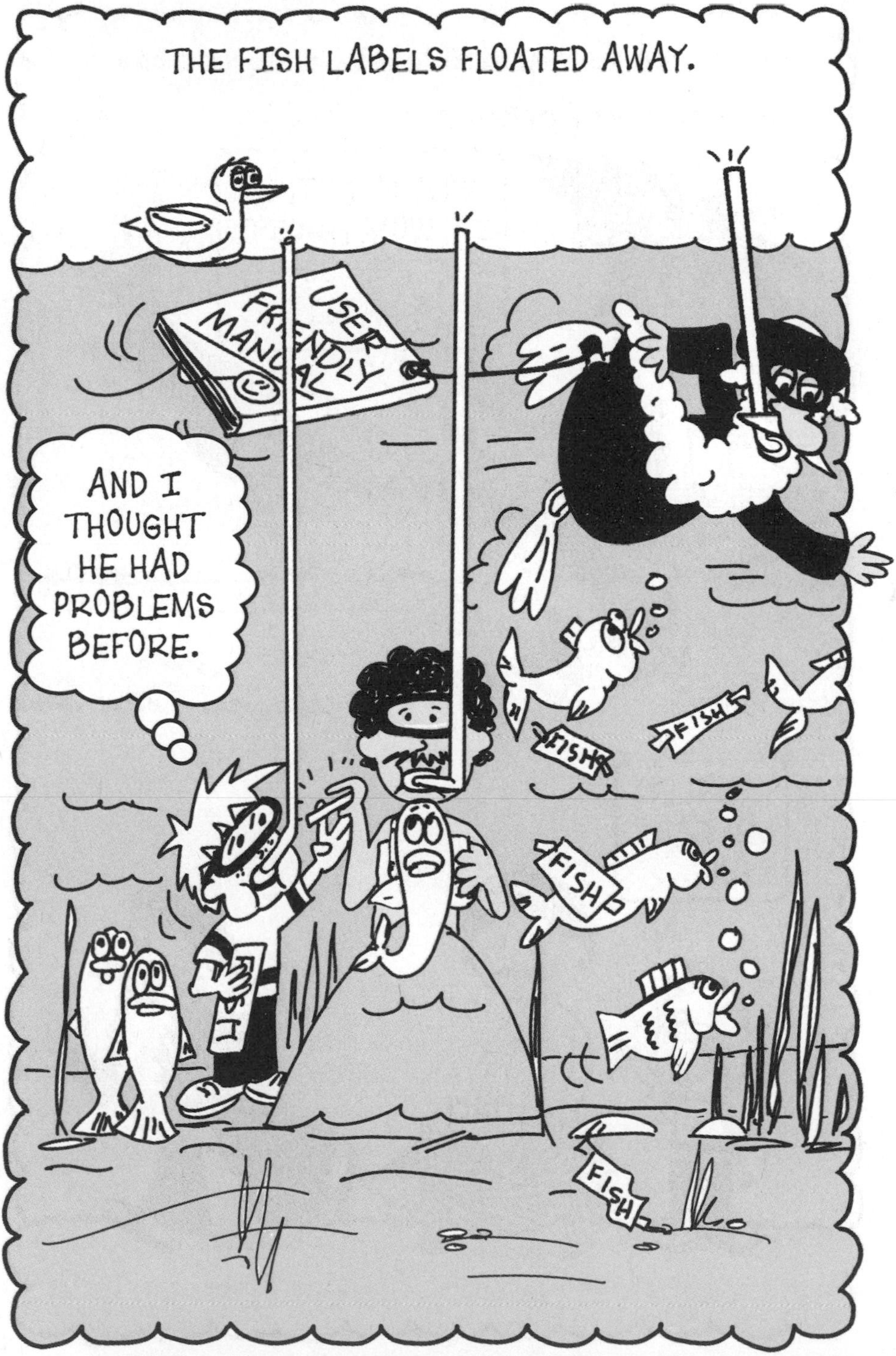
THE FISH LABELS FLOATED AWAY.
USER FRIENDLY MANUAL
AND I THOUGHT HE HAD PROBLEMS BEFORE.
FISH
FISH
FISH
FISH

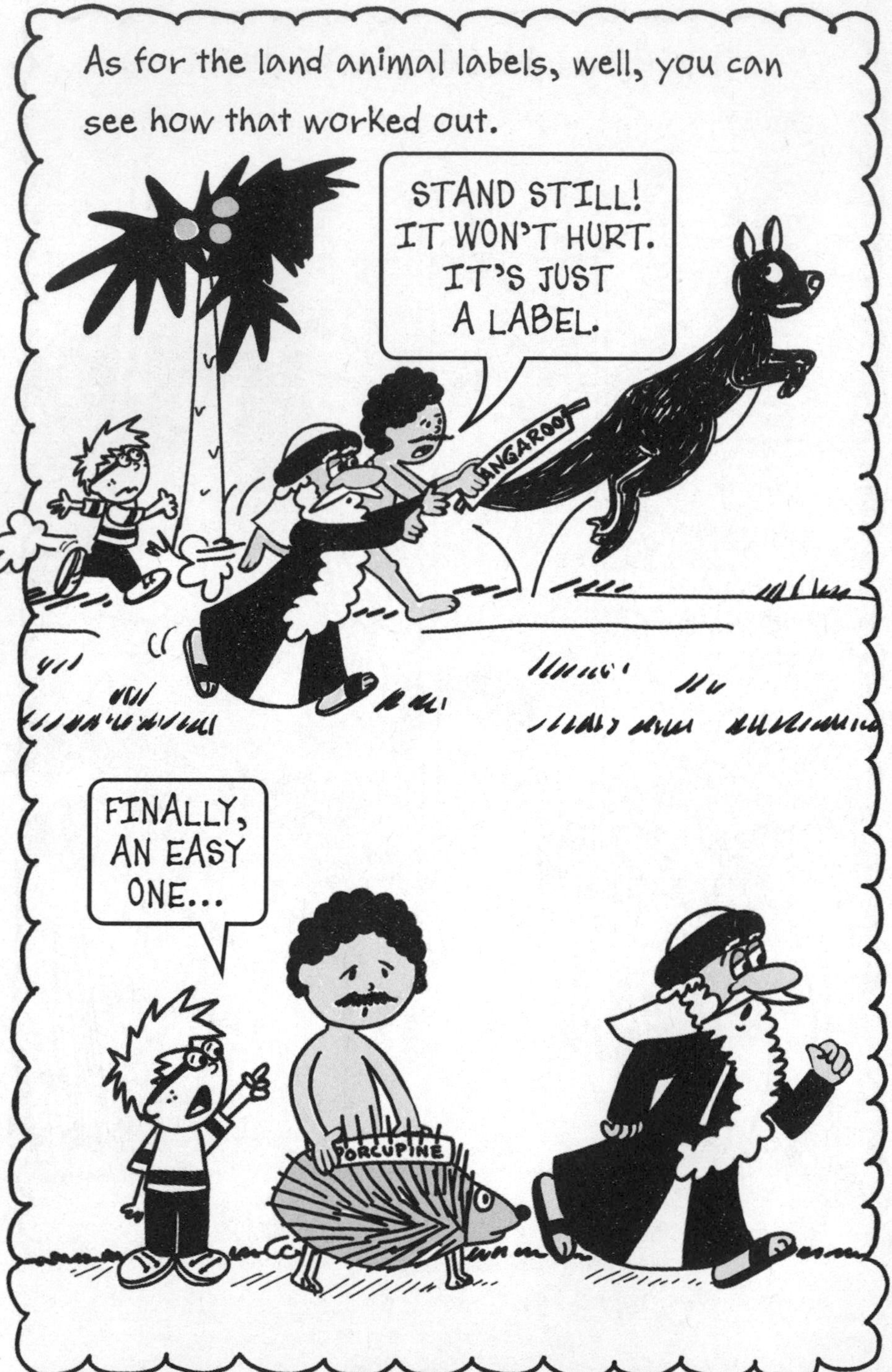
As for the land animal labels, well, you can see how that worked out.
STAND STILL! IT WON'T HURT. IT'S JUST A LABEL.
KANGAROO
FINALLY, AN EASY ONE...
PORCUPINE

All this labeling took forever. When I thought we were done, God brought along one more...

We were all so tired by then we were happy for what came next on Day 7.

See Genesis 1:1–2:25

In case you haven't noticed, I'm drawing a special bubble around my Bible adventure.

TUESDAY...

There's something funny about sleep and me. I told you before, I'm a sleepwalker. But that's not the bad news—the bad news is I TALK in my sleep!

When Marlee figured that out, she installed a video camera right outside my room. A motion sensor turned the camera on when I walked by.

I CAN'T WAIT TO SEE WHAT MY BIG BROTHER IS UP TO ON HIS LATE-NIGHT RAMBLES.

Last week she recorded my cookie jar raid.

Naturally, Marlee spilled the beans!

This morning, however, she was puzzled by the newest video. No way could she know I was dreaming about my Bible adventure.

2:36 A.M.

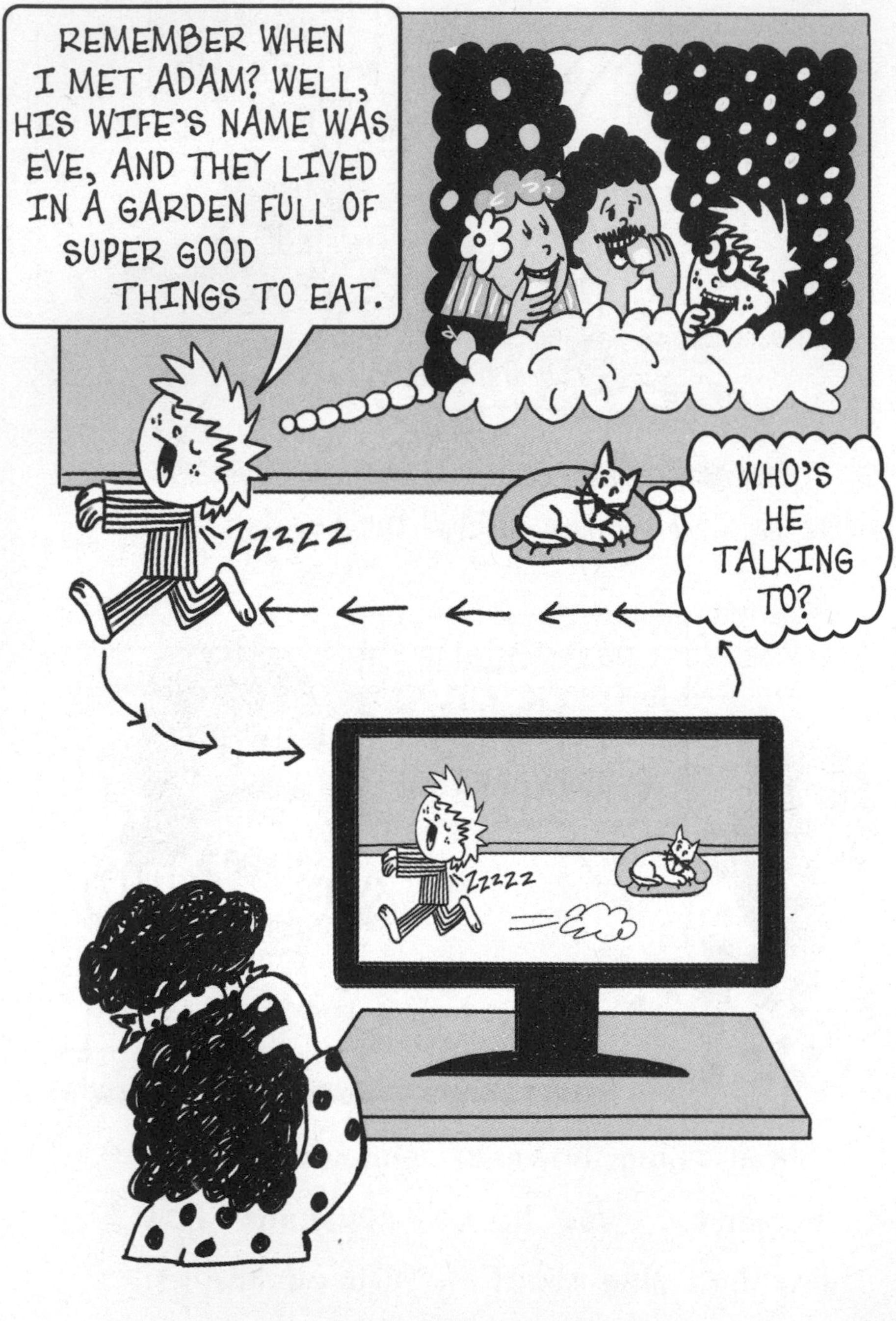
REMEMBER WHEN I MET ADAM? WELL, HIS WIFE'S NAME WAS EVE, AND THEY LIVED IN A GARDEN FULL OF SUPER GOOD THINGS TO EAT.
ZZZZZ
WHO'S HE TALKING TO?
ZZZZZ

2:37 A.M.

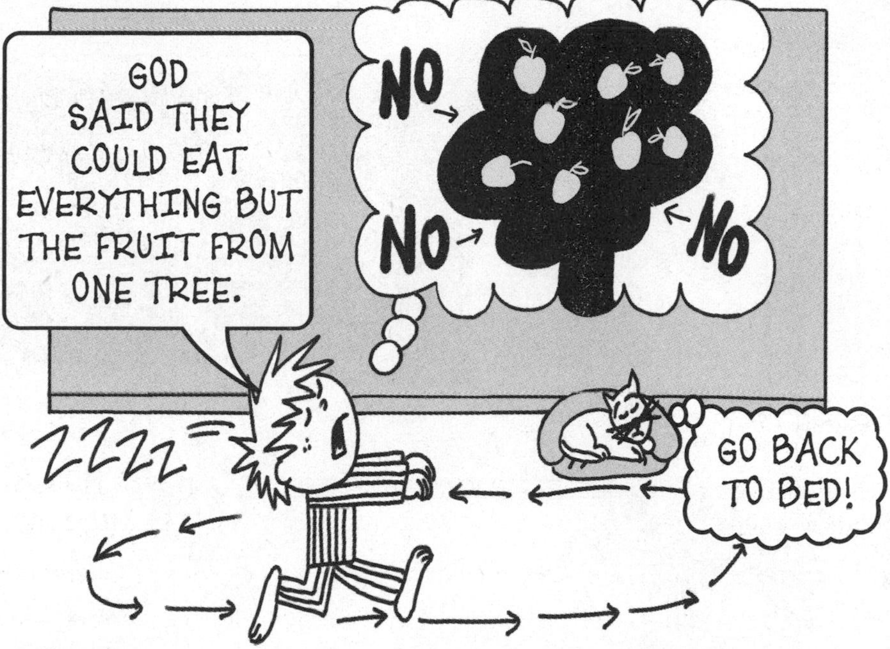
GOD SAID THEY COULD EAT EVERYTHING BUT THE FRUIT FROM ONE TREE.
NO
NO
NO
ZZZZ
GO BACK TO BED!

2:38 A.M.

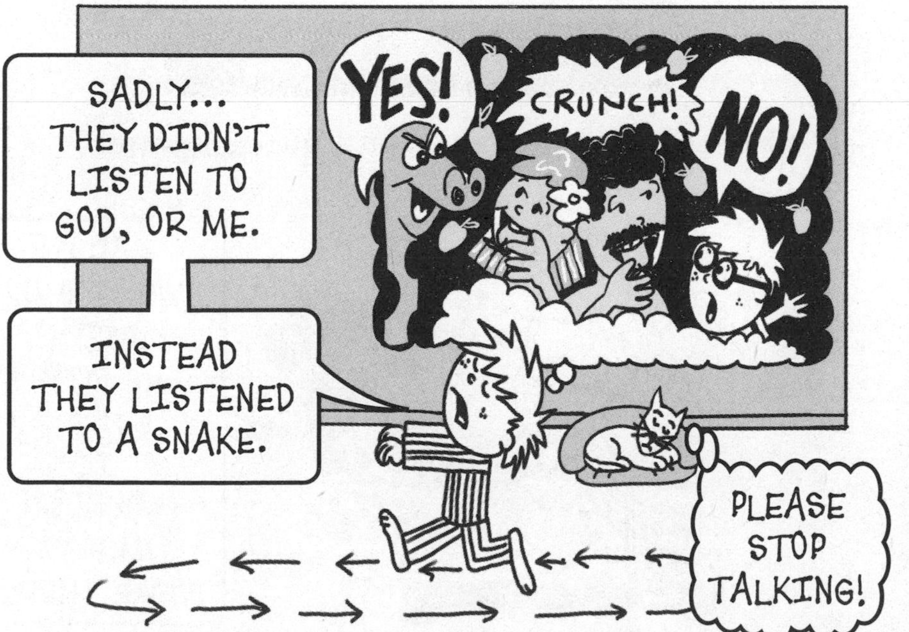
SADLY... THEY DIDN'T LISTEN TO GOD, OR ME.
INSTEAD THEY LISTENED TO A SNAKE.
YES!
CRUNCH!
NO!
PLEASE STOP TALKING!

2:39 A.M.

See Genesis 2:7–3:24

At breakfast Marlee began quizzing me.

I had to think fast. Should I let Marlee in on my Bible adventure?

WEDNESDAY...

My best friend, Billy Zwingli, is the unofficial 4th grade double-barreled spit wad champion.

Today at school, Billy taught me EVERYTHING he knows. Too bad I wasn't listening and nodded off when he got to the part about "how NOT to get caught."

I also missed the part where Billy said, "Spit wads are impossible to scrape off a whiteboard!"

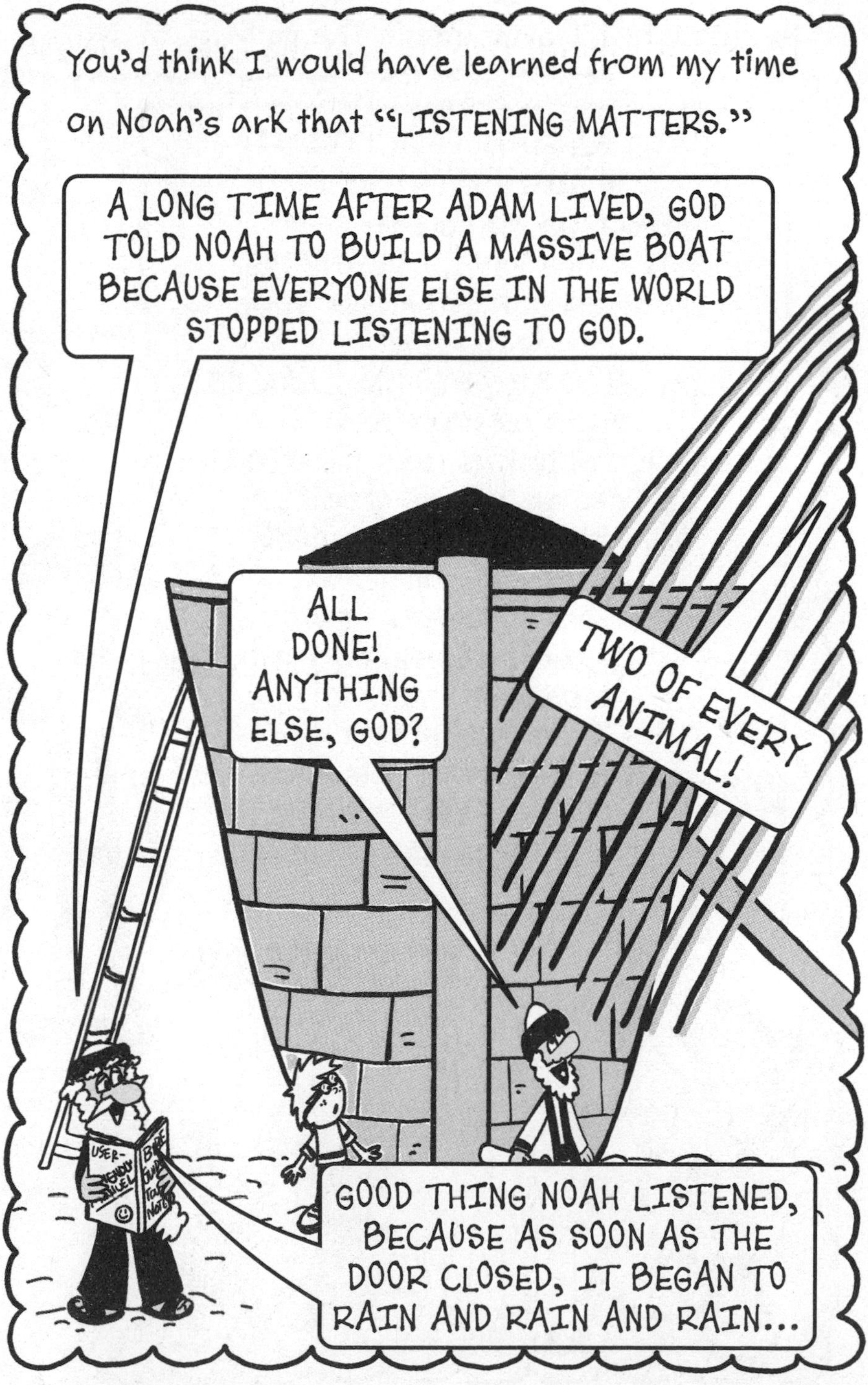
You'd think I would have learned from my time on Noah's ark that "LISTENING MATTERS."
A LONG TIME AFTER ADAM LIVED, GOD TOLD NOAH TO BUILD A MASSIVE BOAT BECAUSE EVERYONE ELSE IN THE WORLD STOPPED LISTENING TO GOD.
ALL DONE! ANYTHING ELSE, GOD?
TWO OF EVERY ANIMAL!
GOOD THING NOAH LISTENED, BECAUSE AS SOON AS THE DOOR CLOSED, IT BEGAN TO RAIN AND RAIN AND RAIN...

Here's what I saw inside the ark...

DAILY SCHEDULE OF ACTIVITIES
5:30 A.M. - EVERYONE UP.
ESPECIALLY YOU SLEEPY BEARS.
6:00 A.M. - FAMILY DEVOTIONS.
SPECIES SPECIFIC TRANSLATIONS
AVAILABLE.
8:00 A.M., 12:00 P.M., 6:00 P.M. - MEALTIMES
BIRDS ON UPPER DECK.
ANIMALS WEIGHING LESS THAN 500LB
ON THE MIDDLE DECK.
BIG BOYS ON THE LOWER DECK.
10:00 A.M. - EXERCISE.
AARDVARKS - NORFOLK TERRIERS
(MON/WED/FRI);
OPOSSUMS - ZEBRAS
(TUES/THURS/SAT).
FLIERS CAN TAKE THEIR PICK.
8:00 P.M. - LAMPS OUT!
YOU NIGHT OWLS, KEEP IT DOWN.

YOU GETTING ALL THIS?

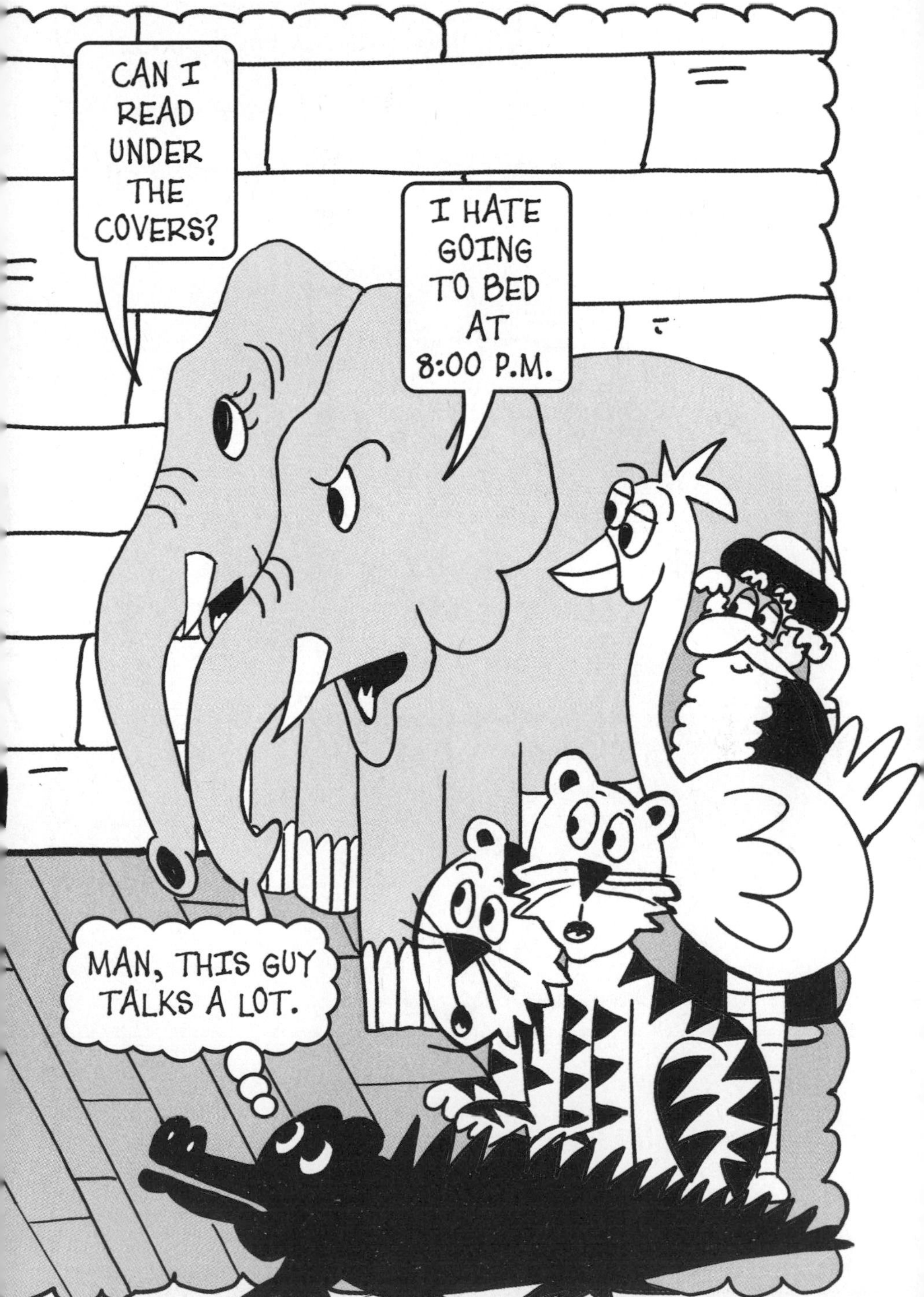
CAN I READ UNDER THE COVERS?
I HATE GOING TO BED AT 8:00 P.M.
MAN, THIS GUY TALKS A LOT.

Most of the animals were good listeners—
that is, except the pigs and the ostriches.
They got their exercise day wrong, messing
EVERYONE UP.

Maybe I should have cut them some slack
because they were probably distracted by
the massive storm raging outside.

By the way, that storm felt like the longest roller-coaster ride EVER. Luckily I LOVE roller coasters.

Moses, on the other hand, couldn't appreciate my enthusiasm.

But the good news was that storm didn't last forever. And we all ended up on top of a mountain.

As you can imagine, everyone was thrilled when it came time to get out.

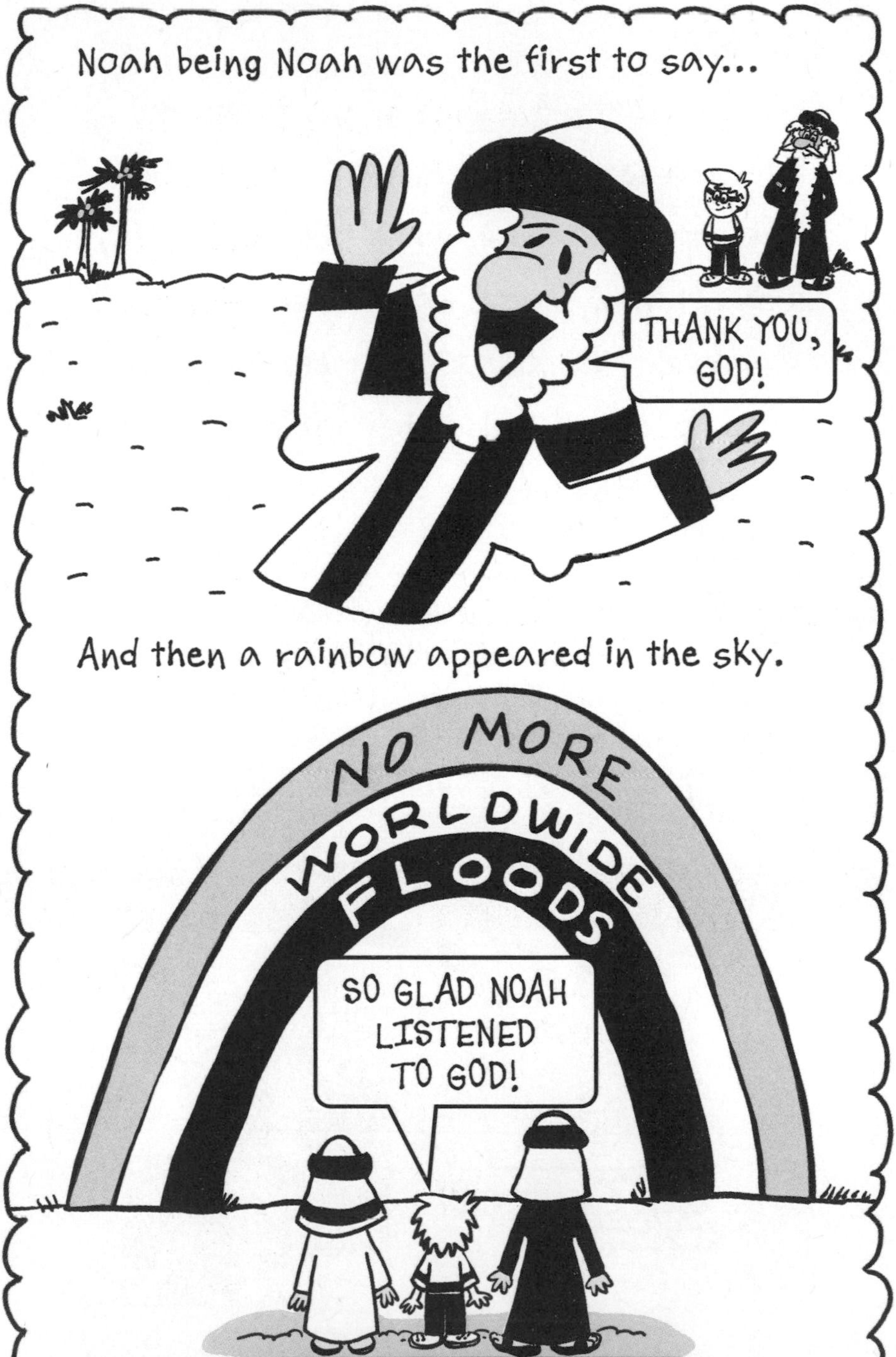
Noah being Noah was the first to say...
THANK YOU, GOD!
And then a rainbow appeared in the sky.
NO MORE WORLDWIDE FLOODS
SO GLAD NOAH LISTENED TO GOD!
See Genesis 6:5–8:22

THURSDAY...

One thing that drives me crazy about my sister Marlee is SHE'S ALWAYS THERE!! So, of course, yesterday while Billy and I played Citycraft in my room with the door CLOSED, IN pranced "NO-KNOCK" Marlee. And even though Billy and I gave her the cold shoulder, she bombarded us with a flood of WORDS!

BET YOU CAN'T CATCH A RAINBOW! THERE'S ONE RIGHT NOW! IT'S BEAUTIFUL AND IT HAS 7 COLORS. I LIKE THE PURPLE COLOR BEST...

IGNORE HER AND SHE'LL GO AWAY!

I CAN TOO CATCH A RAINBOW!

Too late, Billy was already off chasing the rainbow, leaving behind our half-built, AWESOME, STATE-OF-THE-ART, TECHNO-GEEK CITYCRAFT city.

Not to be left alone with Marlee, I hopped on my bike and followed.

Turns out catching a rainbow is tricky. The
faster we rode, the more the rainbow moved.

RAINBOW WAS HERE!

THEN HERE!

THEN HERE!

But our chase was not a TOTAL LOSS. After
17 minutes of exhausting pedaling, Billy and
I spotted the Paradise Ice Cream Parlor.

WELCOME TO
PARADISE

SPECIAL
TODAY

RAINBOW
SHERBET

I guess you could say we caught a rainbow.
THREE SCOOPS!

SATURDAY...

It's the weekend! Time to write about my tower of Babel adventure.

Remember how Noah OBEYED God and built the ark? Well, his great-great-grandkids DISOBEYED God. After the flood, God told the people to spread out all over the EARTH, but instead they stayed put and built A BIG TOWER.

FILL THE EARTH!

NO THANKS, WE LIKE IT HERE!

Mom says Billy's coming over in 15 minutes, so here's a quick cartoon of what I saw...

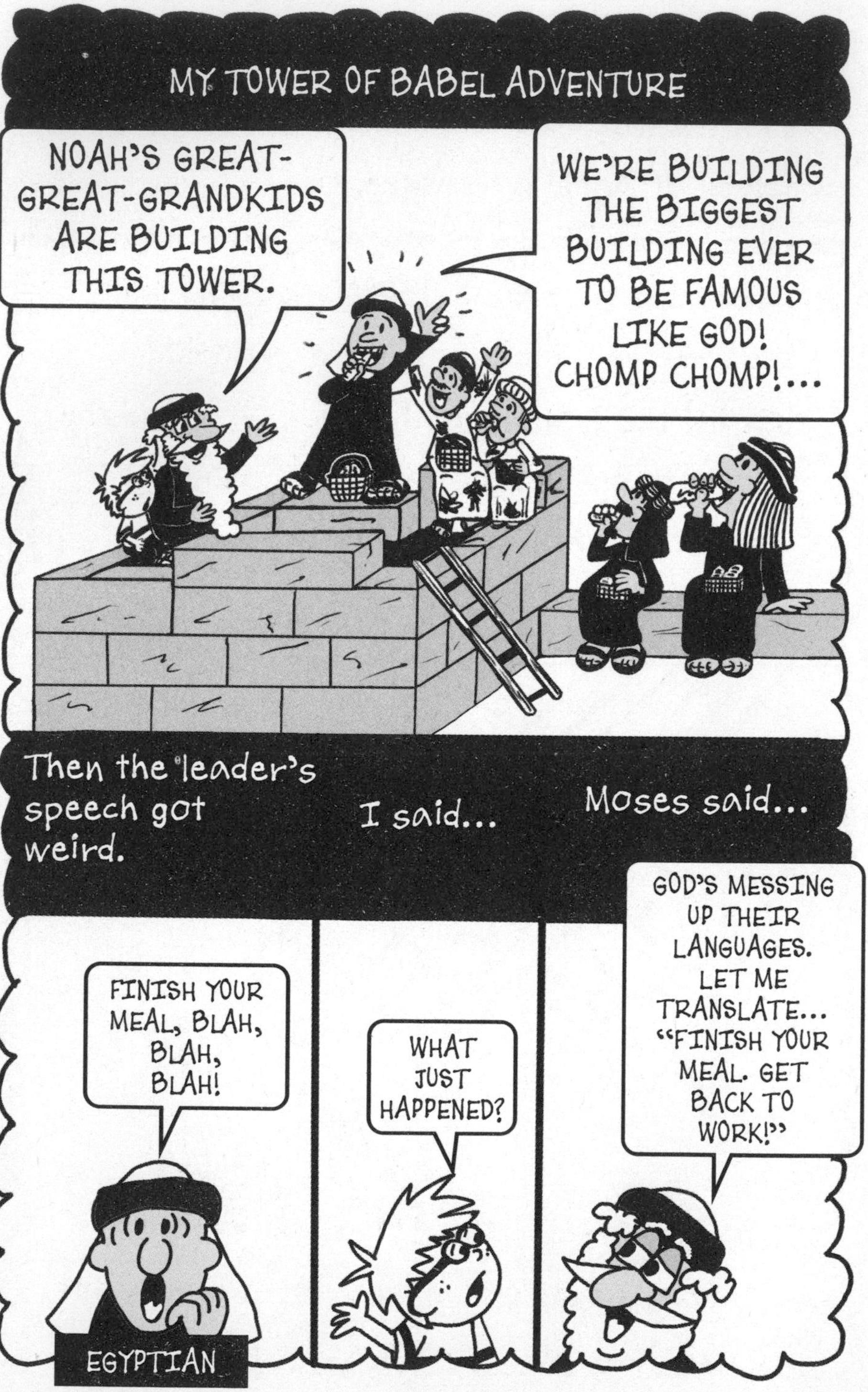
MY TOWER OF BABEL ADVENTURE
NOAH'S GREAT-GREAT-GRANDKIDS ARE BUILDING THIS TOWER.
WE'RE BUILDING THE BIGGEST BUILDING EVER TO BE FAMOUS LIKE GOD! CHOMP CHOMP!...
Then the leader's speech got weird.
I said...
Moses said...
FINISH YOUR MEAL, BLAH, BLAH, BLAH!
EGYPTIAN
WHAT JUST HAPPENED?
GOD'S MESSING UP THEIR LANGUAGES. LET ME TRANSLATE... "FINISH YOUR MEAL. GET BACK TO WORK!"

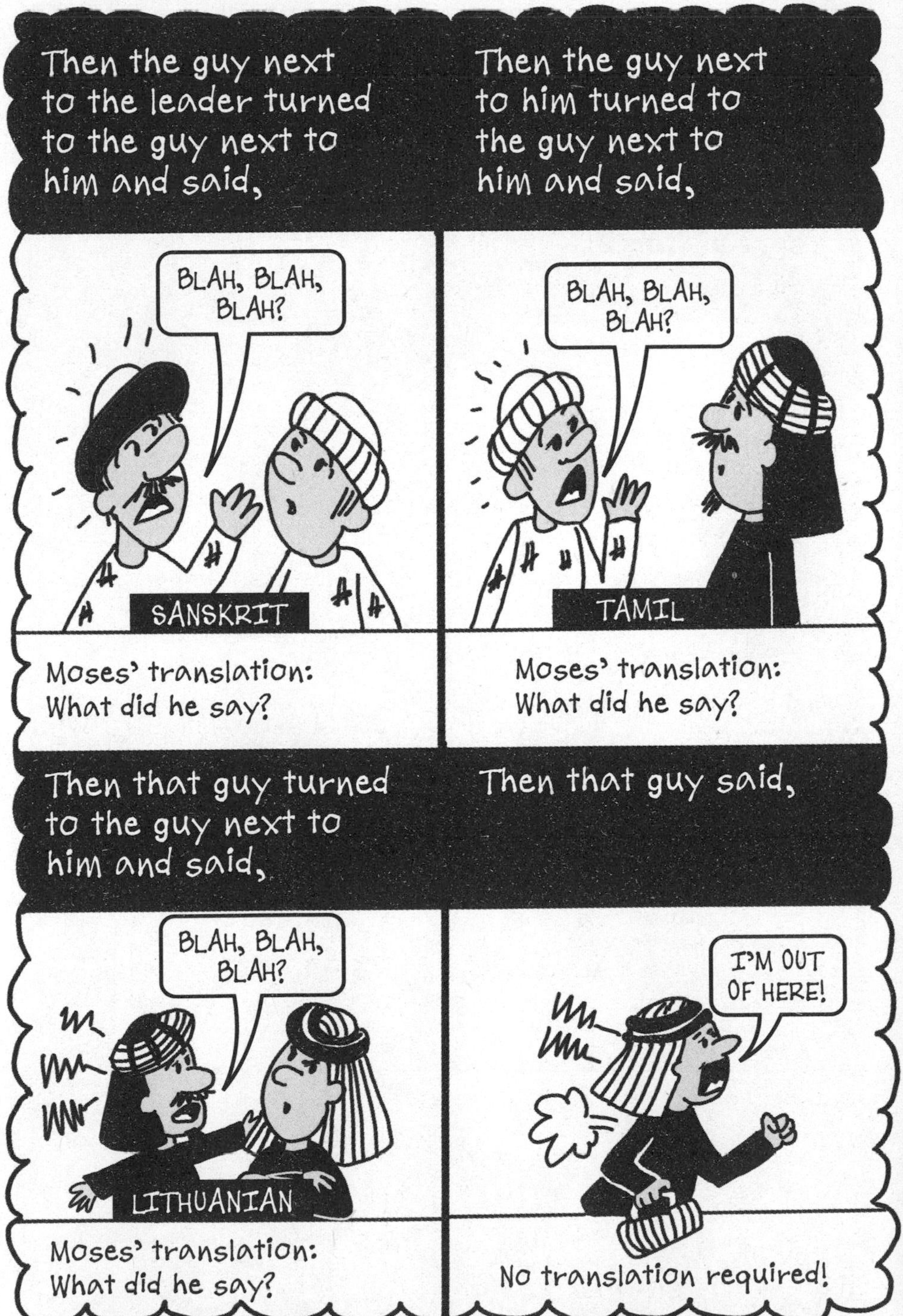
Then the guy next to the leader turned to the guy next to him and said,
BLAH, BLAH, BLAH?
SANSKRIT
Moses' translation: What did he say?
Then the guy next to him turned to the guy next to him and said,
BLAH, BLAH, BLAH?
TAMIL
Moses' translation: What did he say?
Then that guy turned to the guy next to him and said,
BLAH, BLAH, BLAH?
LITHUANIAN
Moses' translation: What did he say?
Then that guy said,
I'M OUT OF HERE!
No translation required!

Finally, like angry hornets, ALL THE GUYS swarmed past me, pushing their way outside. Moses called it...

"THE TANTRUM AT THE TOWER!"

See Genesis 11:1-9

CRAZY STORY, RIGHT? BASICALLY I GOT TO SEE EVERYONE SPREAD OUT ALL OVER THE EARTH JUST LIKE GOD WANTED IN THE FIRST PLACE.

But this God story also has an extra blessing for me in my world today. For when...

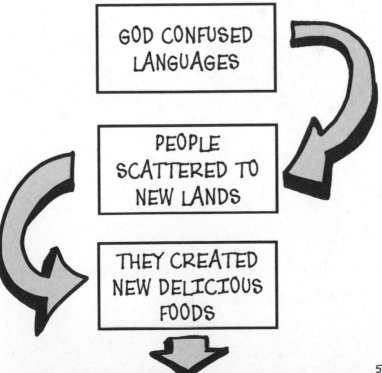

GOD CONFUSED LANGUAGES

PEOPLE SCATTERED TO NEW LANDS

THEY CREATED NEW DELICIOUS FOODS

AND EVENTUALLY
THE MEGA MALL INTERNATIONAL FOOD COURT
WAS BORN!

THE END!

PHEW! Billy's late. YAY! Just enough time to
MICROWAVE A BURRITO.

TUESDAY...

I'm so excited. Dad finally told me I could build a FORT in our big OAK TREE. I knew the perfect spot at the same height as my SLACK LINE. It was not nearly as high as the tower of Babel, which is probably a good thing considering how that turned out.

Dad also offered to help me build it. As an eye doctor, I wasn't sure he could be much help. Unless, of course, I accidentally poked out my eye.

But Dad surprised me. It turned out he was
VERY handy. First, he made a DETAILED MODEL
out of Popsicle sticks.

Then he put up the money.

He even helped frame the platform, walls, and roof.

Once Dad went back to work, Billy became my new wingman.

Remind me to make this tree fort a tech-free zone!

Finally, I was done. Well, almost, till I realized I needed to add one more thing.

SATURDAY...

UGHHH!!! My new tree fort got TP'd. WHAT'S WORSE, since it rained like crazy last night, the toilet paper's stuck on everything like glue.

THANK YOU, DERRICK NEWTON!!!

How do I know this TP job was the handiwork of Derrick Newton? Check out the evidence...

1. Easy night access. He lives next door.

DERRICK'S HOUSE

MY HOUSE

2. His mom buys toilet paper by the pallet.

I LOVE PALLET PRICES!

SEE

3. I once saw him researching at GASKET'S USED BOOKSTORE.

THE DUMMY'S GUIDE TO TP-ING

Still NOT convinced? Here's more evidence...

Age 3: my wagon.

Age 5: my roller skates.

Age 8: my bike.

I'm sad to say Mom and Dad aren't clued in. It probably doesn't help that they are best friends with Derrick's parents.

THE NICEST PEOPLE EVER!

Here's our neighborhood on Mrs. Newton's baking day.

It's MIND-BOGGLING to think Derrick is their kid. His rotten attitude must have come from someone else in his family tree. Probably a creative bank robber who was so bored in his jail cell that he invented TP-ing.

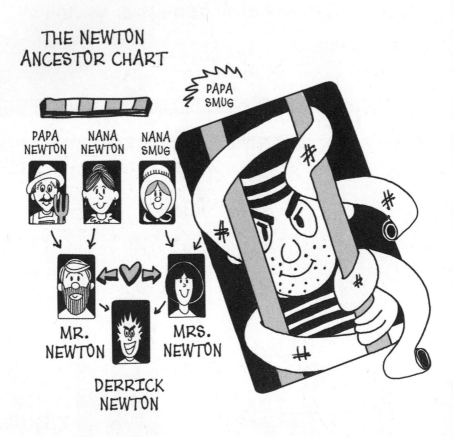

THE NEWTON ANCESTOR CHART

PAPA SMUG

PAPA NEWTON   NANA NEWTON   NANA SMUG

MR. NEWTON   MRS. NEWTON

DERRICK NEWTON

To be honest, I've never ACTUALLY caught Derrick in the act.

But I will...just you wait. Right after I finish cleaning up this MESS.

MONDAY...
Today I had to PAY UP on Dad's ONE CONDITION for letting me build my tree fort. The "NO GIRLS ALLOWED" sign TEMPORARILY came down. Mom and Marlee got their 6-minute tree fort tour. Marlee immediately put in her two cents.

According to Marlee, my tree fort needs
4 bean bags, a SHAG RUG, a tea set, and
artwork.

I reminded her that watching 2 seasons
of "TREE FORT TRANSFORMATIONS" hardly
qualifies her as an expert.

She did get me wondering if I should hang
something on the walls. Of course, it would
have to be MANLY. Maybe a few old photos of
relatives who ROUGHED IT!

Although I don't see any photos of those types of family members hanging in our hallway.

Too bad my cell phone didn't work on my Bible adventure. I could have taken photos of plenty of people living off the land.

After all, Moses said EVERYONE is a descendant of Adam and Eve, so that means EVERYONE I met on my Bible adventure was a distant relative.

First I would have taken a picture of Adam and Eve behind a bush.

See Genesis 2:15-22

Next I would have gotten Noah and his wife and their 3 sons and their wives all lined up in front of the ark.

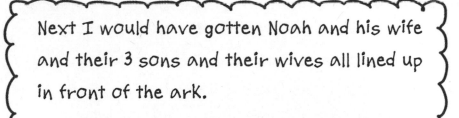

And I definitely would have wanted a photo with Noah's descendants Abraham and Sarah. They REALLY roughed it living in tents their whole lives.

At the age of 90, Sarah even had a baby boy in a TENT.

But then again, even if my camera had worked, I wouldn't have had time to snap a picture as I was too busy changing baby Isaac's diapers.

PATRICK, YOUR TURN TO CHANGE HIM.

BETTER HIM THAN ME!

See Genesis 18:1-15; 21:1-7

Anyway...since I don't have any photos
of those Bible relatives, this afternoon
I decided to draw their portraits for my
tree fort walls. I also decided to get some
tree fort furniture. What do you think?

It's amazing the deals you can get at the
DUMP.

Oh, and in case you were wondering, I also updated my sign.

SUNDAY...

Moms can be SO UNCOOL! Especially when your mom is your Sunday school teacher and she constantly uses YOUR LIFE as an object lesson.

ME INCOGNITO AT SUNDAY SCHOOL!

Take today. Mom held up some of our hallway family photos and said...

PATRICK, PLEASE TELL EVERYONE WHO THESE FOLKS ARE.

WELCOME

DIED OF EMBARRASSMENT IN SUNDAY SCHOOL!

Unfazed by my theatrics, Mom continued, "You probably all have family photos in your house. But I'll bet you didn't know that you're also a member of a larger family that began in the first book of the Bible, called Genesis."

Since everyone looked confused, she pulled out some drawings of Bible characters. Take it from me, they looked NOTHING like what I saw.

WHAT I SAW

MOSES - EVE - ADAM
ABRAHAM - SARAH

MOM'S PICTURE

MOSES - EVE - ADAM
ABRAHAM - SARAH

Of course, I kept my mouth shut about the accuracy of HER cartoons. But suddenly I realized...

MOM MUST BE READING MY JOURNAL!! I just wrote about the "I'm part of God's family" topic, and today she taught on it. That can't be a COINCIDENCE! Time to beef up my security. I'll put my journal under the dirty laundry, under my bed.

NO, that's not enough! I'll hide it inside a trunk, chained and locked with a 2-inch steel Master 5LF lock, under the dirty laundry, under my bed.

STILL NOT ENOUGH! I'll put a "DO NOT DISTURB" labeled chest inside the trunk, chained and locked with a 2-inch steel Master 5LF lock, under the dirty laundry, under my bed.

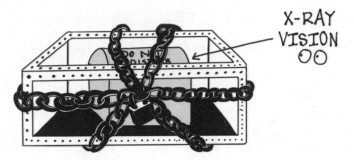

X-RAY VISION OO

BETTER! BUT JUST TO BE ULTRA-CAREFUL, I'm going to top it all off by putting it inside Dad's old stinky sock, inside a chest, inside the trunk, chained and locked with a 2-inch steel Master 5LF lock, under the dirty laundry, under my bed.

DOUBLE X-RAY VISION OO

Now when Mom goes on her Saturday night prowls for Sunday school lesson ideas, she'll NEVER find my journal.

And even though I probably should be flattered if Mom IS taking ideas from my journal, I'm not ready to share it with the world yet. I want to have it ALL written down and thought through because I know there are going to be tons of questions.

THURSDAY...

I had the SCARIEST NIGHTMARE last night.
I dreamed that Derrick Newton brainwashed
Billy into joining his secret club.

In the dream I was spying outside Derrick's
clubhouse, trying to figure out a way to
rescue Billy. Then I discovered a hidden
intercom under the front doormat...

Suddenly, my dream took a turn for the worse. A giant green hand

through the intercom and grabbed me by the throat. That's when I woke up in a cold sweat.

I remember on my Bible adventure, a guy named Jacob told me about HIS strange dream.

ONE NIGHT, WHILE CAMPING IN THE DESERT, I DREAMED ABOUT HEAVEN, STAIRS, AND ANGELS WALKING UP AND DOWN.

COOL!

YES, COOL! WHATEVER THAT MEANS.

AND PATRICK, JUST IN CASE YOU'RE WONDERING, JACOB WAS THE GRANDSON OF ABRAHAM AND SARAH.

WHOOSH! Then suddenly I ended up IN that dream Jacob just told me about, standing on a floating staircase that reached all the way up to heaven. A cheerful line of angels walked up and down past me. One BUMP would have instantly sent me overboard as there were NO HANDRAILS!

ON YOUR RIGHT!

HEAVEN

PATRICK, JUST WAIT— MY DREAM GETS CRAZIER.

Then God SPOKE to Jacob in his dream.

Mom says it's rude to eavesdrop on other people's conversations. But REALLY, what's a kid to do when you're stuck in someone else's dream?

See Genesis 28:10-15

SATURDAY...

I LOVE CAKE. This afternoon, Mom's Sunday school helper, Jenna, got married. Mom brought home a HUGE SLICE of the leftover wedding cake. Talk about RAKING IT IN! And I didn't even have to go to the wedding.

Billy and I met in my tree fort for the feast. I invited my other best friend, Simon, too. He wanted to come, but he said he was on a MISSION!

Simon's a genius. He's always busy in his lab concocting his newest brainy invention. He's so focused he sometimes forgets to EAT.

We missed him! But at least there was more WEDDING CAKE for us.

A perfect cake feast moment. ALMOST...

...till I flashed back to Jacob's weddings on my Bible adventure. That poor guy had to work SOOOOOOOOOOOOOOOOOOOOOOOO hard for HIS WEDDING CAKE.

Here's what happened...

YOU THOUGHT MY DREAM WAS STRANGE? CHECK OUT MY LOVE STORY. NO JUDGMENT, OK?

SURE, NO JUDGMENT.

I had no idea how hard that would be.

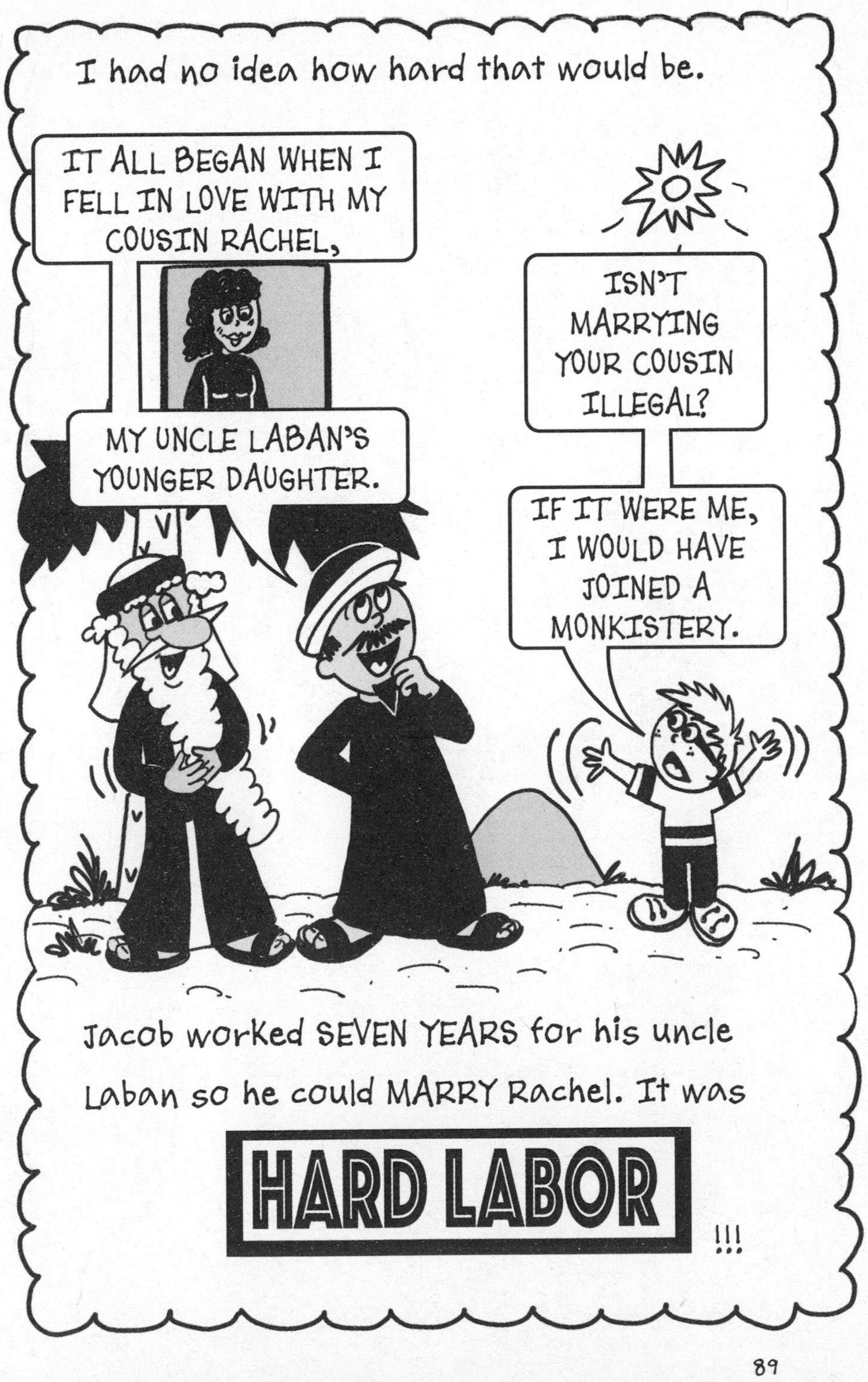
IT ALL BEGAN WHEN I FELL IN LOVE WITH MY COUSIN RACHEL,
MY UNCLE LABAN'S YOUNGER DAUGHTER.
ISN'T MARRYING YOUR COUSIN ILLEGAL?
IF IT WERE ME, I WOULD HAVE JOINED A MONKISTERY.

Jacob worked SEVEN YEARS for his uncle Laban so he could MARRY Rachel. It was

HARD LABOR !!!

That's when I told Jacob one of Dad's favorite quotes. "Love is blind!"

Dad likes to collect quotes related to eyes because he's an eye doctor.

By the way, if you think the word

OPHTHALMÔLÔGIST

is strange and hard to explain in OUR world,
try BIBLE times.

AN OPHTHALMOLOGIST DOES SURGERY ON SICK EYES.

SURGERY IS WHEN THEY CUT OPEN THE EYE TO MAKE IT HEALTHY AGAIN.

GROSS!

Turns out, on Jacob's wedding day, instead of giving his younger daughter, Rachel, to Jacob, Uncle Laban gave him his older daughter, Leah. Jacob didn't have a clue.

That convinced me that Dad's quote needs to be expanded. "Love makes you...

DEAF...

AND BLIND."

DEAF...Why couldn't Jacob tell by Leah's "I DO!" voice that she wasn't Rachel?

BLIND...Well, in Jacob's defense, I wouldn't have noticed the switch either. Especially since he said the bride wore so many clothes, he could barely tell she was human.

Then Jacob said, "Once I realized I married Leah, I still wanted to marry RACHEL! So, back to Uncle Laban's hard labor camp for 7 MORE years."

Now, I'm not a math whiz, but I do know that 7+7 = 14. And that 14 is YEARS!! That's when I broke my "no judgment" policy.

YOU HAVE TO BE IN LOVE TO UNDERSTAND.

I doubted I would EVER understand, but I did hope, on Jacob's SECOND wedding day, he asked his bride one very important question BEFORE he said, "I DO!"

SINCE I WILL HAVE TO WORK FOR YOU FOR 7 MORE YEARS, COULD I SEE YOUR CAMEL DRIVER'S LICENSE?

See Genesis 29:1-30

TUESDAY...

I've always felt DIFFERENT from everyone else because of my weird life. BUT on my Bible adventure, Moses told me...

A LOT OF STRANGE THINGS TAKE PLACE IN THE BIBLE. LOOK AT WHAT HAPPENED AFTER JACOB'S TWO WEDDINGS: HIS WIVES HAD A "WHO CAN HAVE THE MOST BABIES COMPETITION."

I'LL GIVE YOU LOTS OF BABIES.

I'LL GIVE YOU MORE.

LEAH   JACOB   RACHEL

"Whoever had the most kids won," continued Moses. "The HIGHLY competitive sisters made up their own rules as they went along. They even gave their maids, Zilpah and Bilhah, to Jacob just so the babies they had counted for each sister."

I felt sorry for Jacob and hoped he had a support group.

HI, MY NAME IS JACOB. I HAVE 2 WIVES AND I'M ALL STRESSED OUT.

MULTI-WIVES SUPPORT GROUP

Then Moses went into MORE DETAIL about the sisters' competition. Good thing he talked slowly, as I had to draw a diagram just to keep the family members straight.

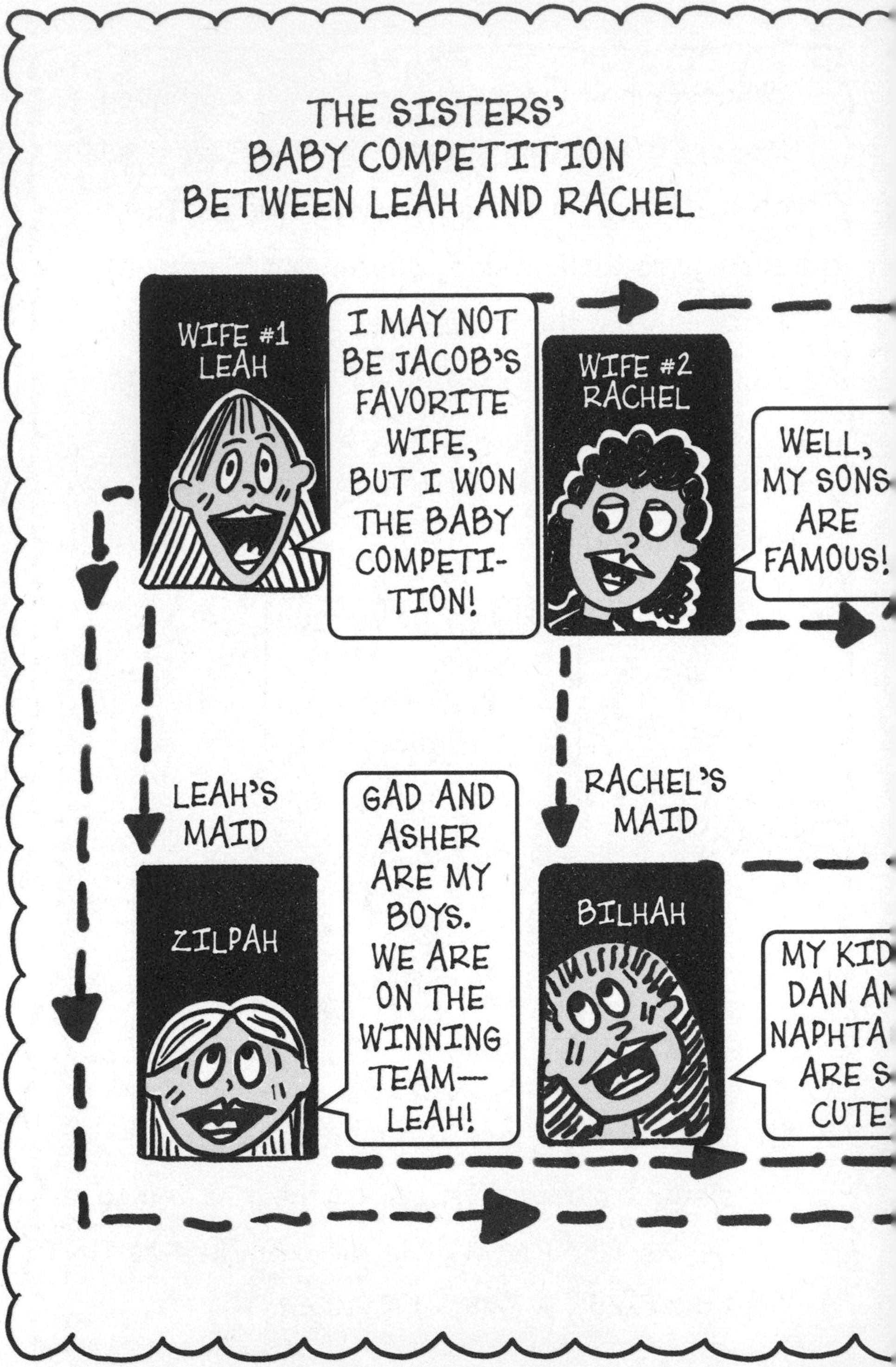
THE SISTERS' BABY COMPETITION BETWEEN LEAH AND RACHEL
WIFE #1 LEAH
I MAY NOT BE JACOB'S FAVORITE WIFE, BUT I WON THE BABY COMPETI-TION!
WIFE #2 RACHEL
WELL, MY SONS ARE FAMOUS!
LEAH'S MAID
ZILPAH
GAD AND ASHER ARE MY BOYS. WE ARE ON THE WINNING TEAM—LEAH!
RACHEL'S MAID
BILHAH
MY KID DAN AN NAPHTA ARE S CUTE

JACOB'S 12 SONS
(AND 1 DAUGHTER)

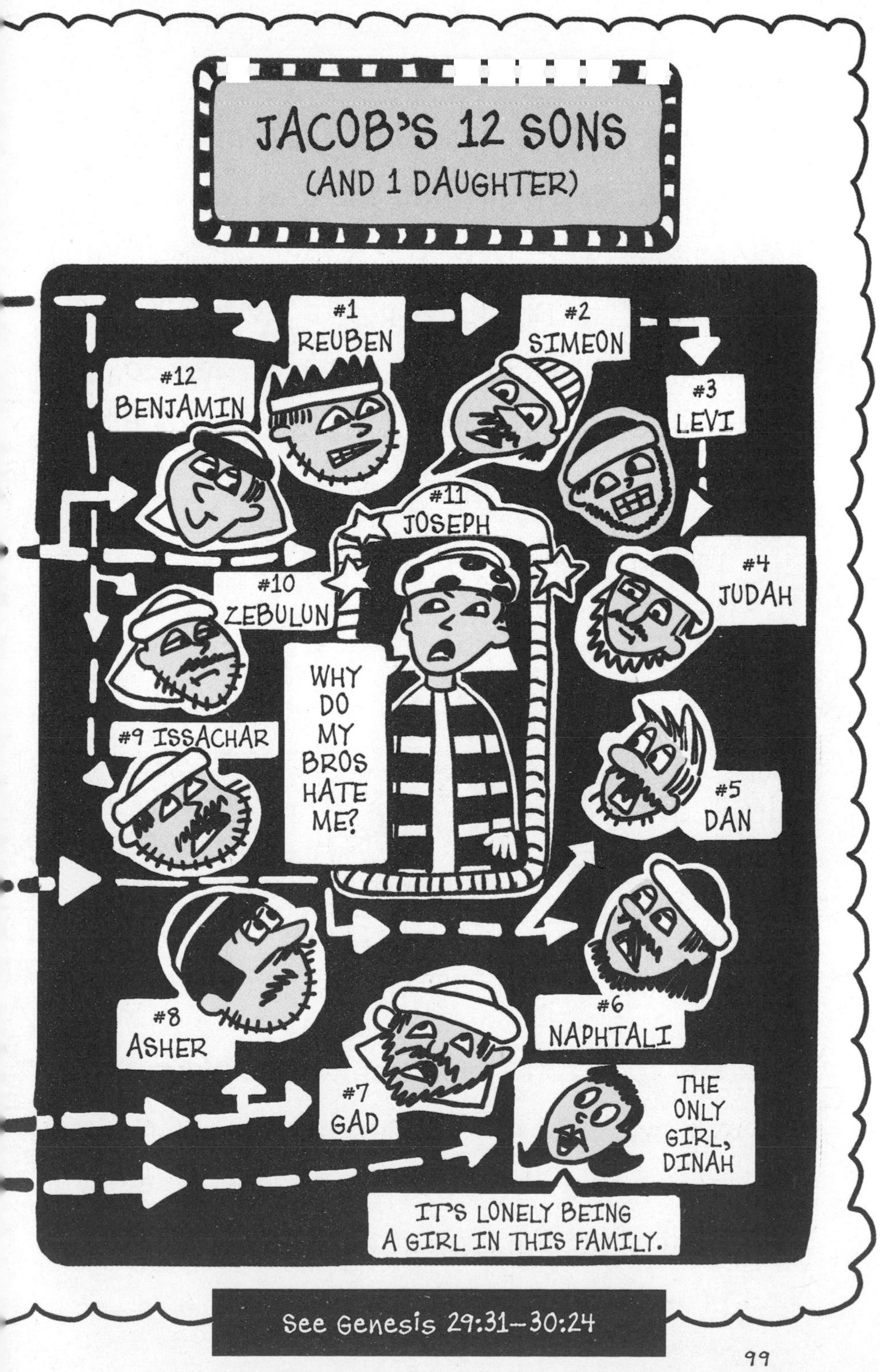
#1 REUBEN
#2 SIMEON
#3 LEVI
#4 JUDAH
#5 DAN
#6 NAPHTALI
#7 GAD
#8 ASHER
#9 ISSACHAR
#10 ZEBULUN
#11 JOSEPH
#12 BENJAMIN
WHY DO MY BROS HATE ME?
THE ONLY GIRL, DINAH
IT'S LONELY BEING A GIRL IN THIS FAMILY.

See Genesis 29:31–30:24

FRIDAY...

Speaking of crazy competitions, you won't believe the one I got into the other day. My cousins were over for a family BBQ. They're ALL GIRLS, so I got to invite Billy and Simon. While everyone else ate hot dogs, hamburgers, chips, and watermelon, we snuck our dinners up to my tree fort.

I NEVER FEEL LONELY WHEN YOU GUYS ARE AROUND! WAIT UP!

CHEF DAD

It only took a few minutes before Simon convinced us to launch our hot dogs like missiles using his newest invention. He even brought along 5 extra packages of hot dogs, just for the occasion.

First, we squirted Ketchup on one side of
the hot dog, mustard on the other side,
and lastly mayonnaise on the tip and tail.

Then we took turns placing two dogs at a
time in Simon's brilliant contraption and sent
them whizzing through space.

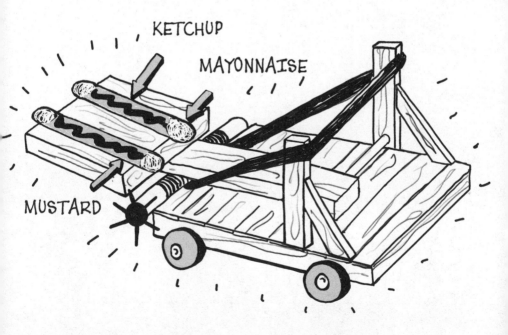

Our intended target was the BULLSEYE on the
other side of my parents' patio.

Simon even provided a score sheet.

HOT DOG MISSILE CONTEST			
	PATRICK	BILLY	SIMON
ACCURACY	0	0	0

We were all super competitive but nobody
could hit the BULLSEYE. Unfortunately, we hit
everything else.

After that, Dad showed us a game of his own. He called it CLEAN UP YOUR MESS.

WEDNESDAY...

What's up with all these bragging parents? Bragging ought to be BANNED! I get the 1st amendment freedom of speech, but they oughta outlaw embarrassing your kids. My friends all agree. Especially when it comes to the Internet.

Last night, Mrs. Zwingli posted a picture of Billy blowing out the candles on his cake.

MY BABY IS 10 YEARS OLD
TODAY. LOVE YOU, HONEY!

Then, this morning, Mr. Stanley posted a picture of Simon holding his newest experiment, with this comment.

104

THE SIGN OF A TRUE GENIUS
IS THEIR WILLINGNESS TO FAIL!

But it's MY MOM who wins the prize for the longest-running embarrassing post. Eight years later, her post "MY SON PATRICK POTTY TRAINED HIMSELF!" is still getting me stopped in the grocery store.

I guess I shouldn't complain. At least my parents' bragging didn't get ME into trouble.

Not like what I saw on the next part of my Bible adventure. Jacob's bragging about his son Joseph ruined Joseph's relationship with his brothers.

GRRRRRRRRRRRRRR GRRRRRRRRRRRRRR

DON'T YOU JUST LOVE THE COAT I GAVE MY FAVORITE SON!

NOT REALLY, IT LOOKS LIKE A BEACH TOWEL!

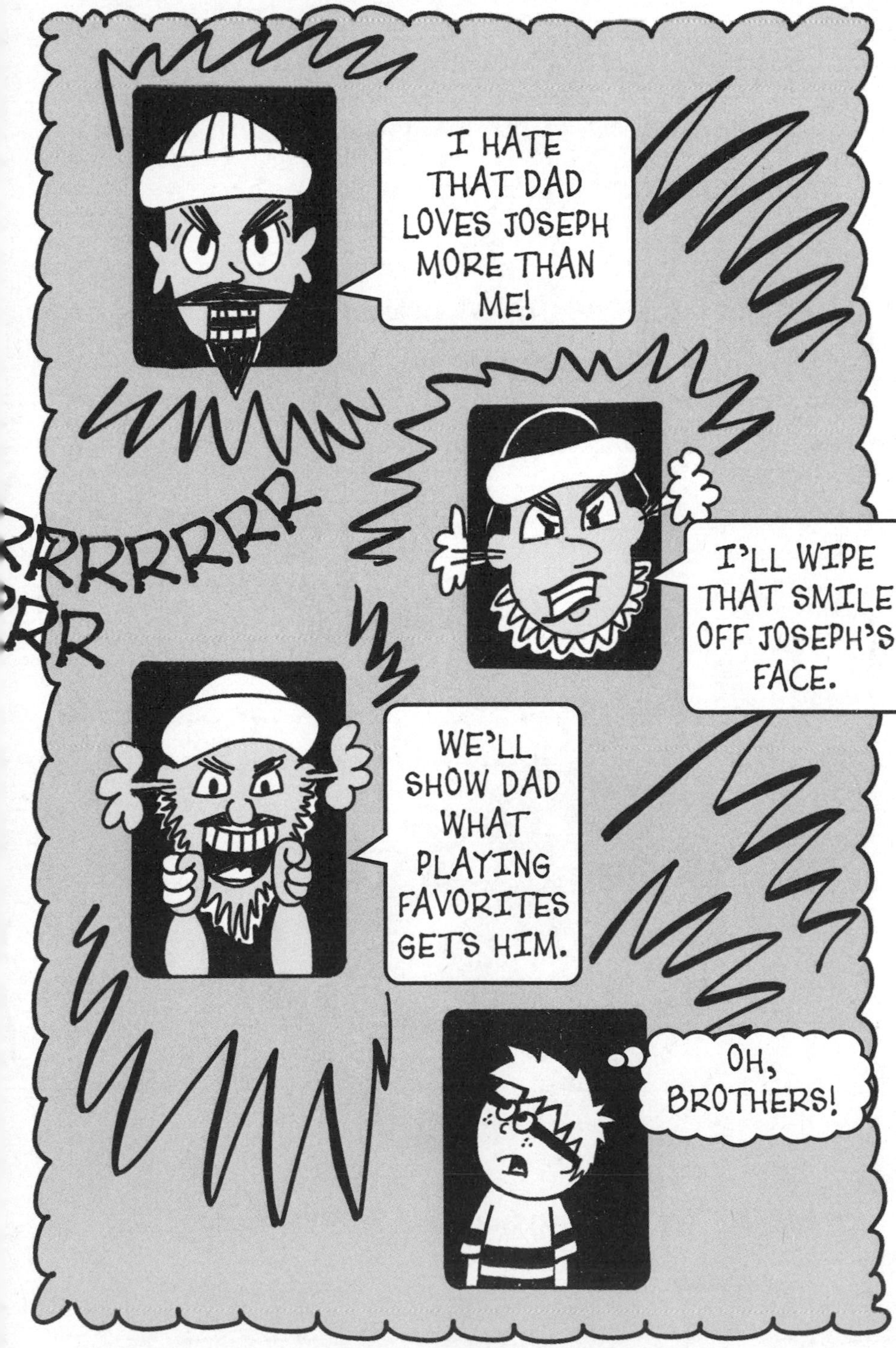
I HATE THAT DAD LOVES JOSEPH MORE THAN ME!
RRRRRRR
RR
I'LL WIPE THAT SMILE OFF JOSEPH'S FACE.
WE'LL SHOW DAD WHAT PLAYING FAVORITES GETS HIM.
OH, BROTHERS!

And that was the reaction of only 3 of the brothers. I could tell hanging out with JOSEPH was going to be hazardous to my health.

Somehow Moses must have read my mind because he SKIPPED OUT of the next part of this story.

SMART GUY—it turned out WORSE than I imagined.

IMMEDIATELY, I got dumped HEADFIRST down a well by those angry brothers, SMACK-DAB on top of Joseph.

Then the brothers sold us to an Egyptian slave trader.

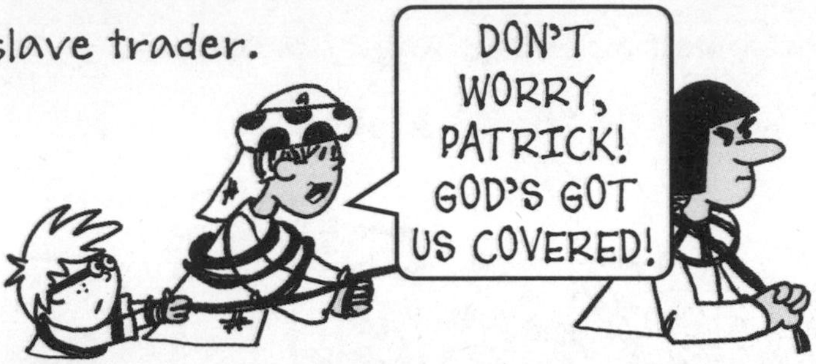
DON'T WORRY, PATRICK! GOD'S GOT US COVERED!

Who sold us to a guy named Potiphar.

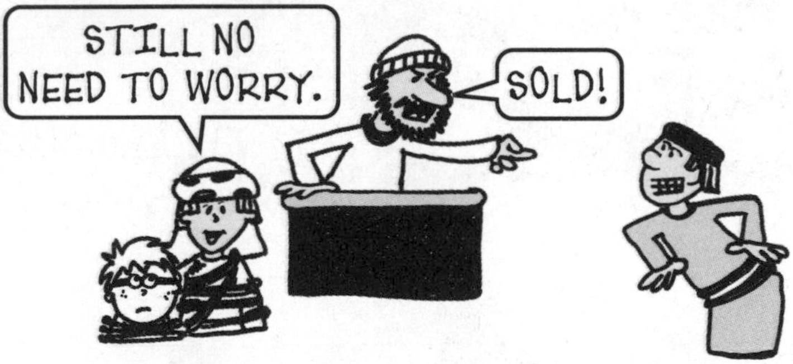
STILL NO NEED TO WORRY.
SOLD!

Who later falsely accused Joseph and had us thrown into an Egyptian jail.

GOOD THING I LIKE STRIPES.

That's when I also decided to make the best of things and tell some PRISON jokes.

Q: WHAT DO PRISONERS USE TO CALL EACH OTHER?

A: CELL PHONES!

Q: WHY DID THE PICTURE GO TO JAIL?

A: BECAUSE IT WAS FRAMED.

I CRACK ME UP!

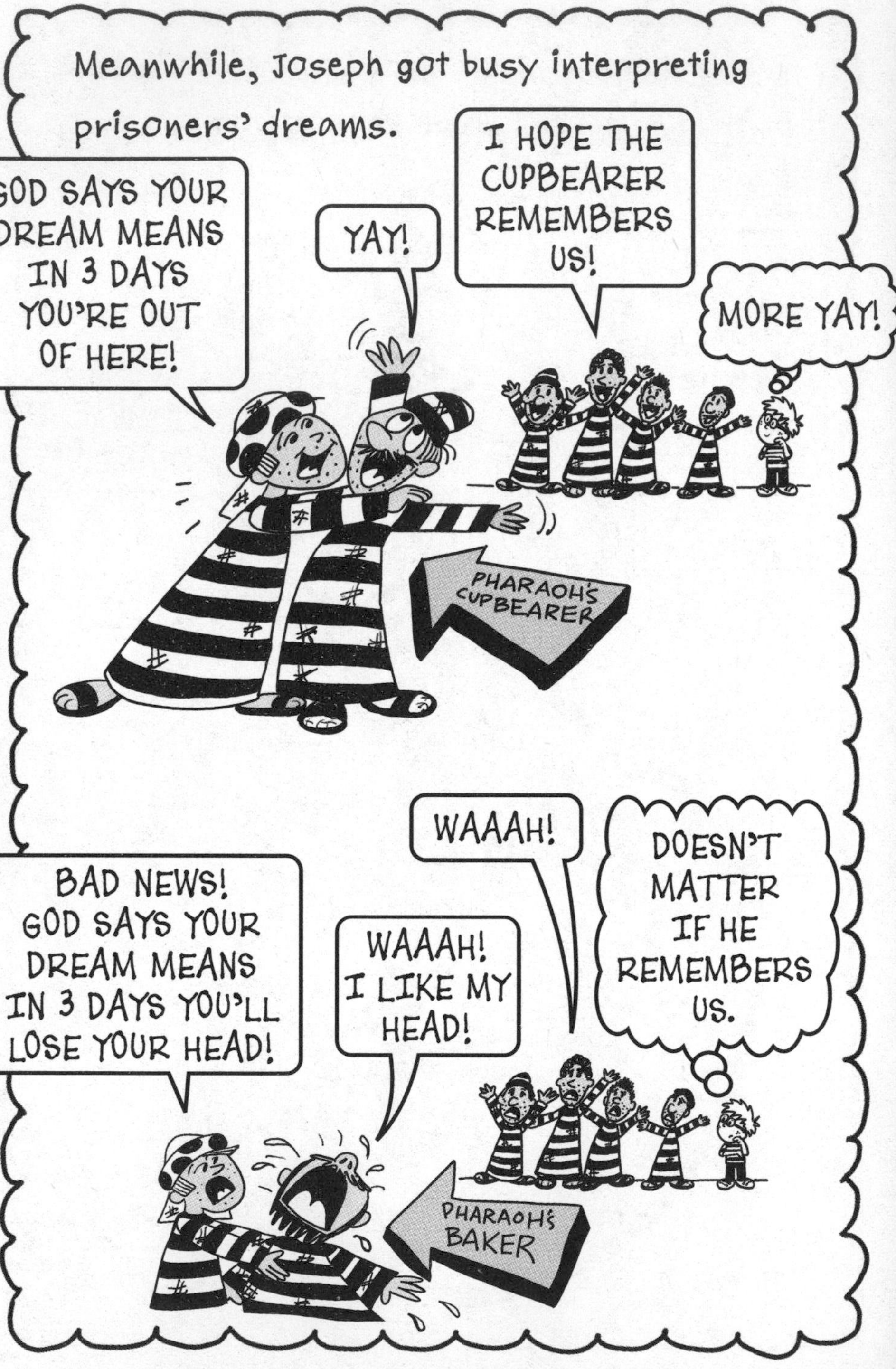
Meanwhile, Joseph got busy interpreting prisoners' dreams.
GOD SAYS YOUR DREAM MEANS IN 3 DAYS YOU'RE OUT OF HERE!
YAY!
I HOPE THE CUPBEARER REMEMBERS US!
MORE YAY!
PHARAOH'S CUPBEARER
BAD NEWS! GOD SAYS YOUR DREAM MEANS IN 3 DAYS YOU'LL LOSE YOUR HEAD!
WAAAH! I LIKE MY HEAD!
WAAAH!
DOESN'T MATTER IF HE REMEMBERS US.
PHARAOH'S BAKER

I didn't mind Joseph stealing the spotlight because after a while it did get us out of jail and into the palace. Turns out Pharaoh had a strange dream, so the cupbearer told him about Joseph and Joseph explained to Pharaoh what the dream meant.

BECAUSE YOU INTERPRETED MY DREAM, I'M GOING TO MAKE YOU SECOND IN COMMAND.

THANK GOD. HE TOLD ME WHAT TO SAY.

KEEP TALKING, JOSEPH, I'M LOVING THIS PALACE FOOD.

See Genesis 37; 39:1–41:44

Note to parents:
Just because Jacob's BRAGGING turned out OK for Joseph, that doesn't get you off the hook. STOP IT!

FRIDAY...

Parents' bragging is not the only way a kid can get in TROUBLE. Sometimes TROUBLE just FINDS you. Take, for example, what happened to me a couple of weeks back in class after a hard test.

Sure, I could have stolen his answers. I had a perfect view of his test.

FOLLOW THE
ARROW

And, SURE, my answers were EXACTLY the same as his.

SCIENCE TEST

But I swear I didn't cheat.

Dad says...

Obviously, I wouldn't want that to happen.

Unfortunately for me, Mrs. McPherson doesn't believe in coincidences. Neither does Principal Potts.

Here's me INSIDE Principal Potts's office
drawing funny cartoons about my not funny
situation.

Fortunately, 2 big breaks happened.
First, the computer of Principal Potts's
administrative assistant, Miss Mars,
went down right when she was making
a flyer for Back to School Night.

So I made her one.

Second, while Miss Mars was telling Principal Potts all about my heroics, he got a phone call from Principal Best of TOP DOG Elementary School regarding the upcoming Mamba Juice poster contest.

I guess you could say timing is EVERYTHING. Immediately after he got off the phone, Principal Potts offered me a deal I coudn't refuse. Maybe he finally believed I didn't cheat.

Here's a mini version of my WINNING poster.

What's more, the GRAND PRIZE, a truck full
of Mamba Juice smoothies, got delivered to
school on the hottest day of the year.

Tonight when Dad asked me what lesson I
learned from the whole situation, it didn't
take me long to think of the answer.

I said, "Bring a good drawing pen to
school, just in case TROUBLE finds you."

TUESDAY...

Bonding time! That's what Billy and I had yesterday. For us, bonding always requires an extra-large box of CHOCOLATE CHIP COOKIES.

WITHOUT COOKIES!   WITH COOKIES!

All I know is they're the magic ingredient for talking up a storm. By the way, COOKIE BONDING is way more fun than PAIN BONDING.

The book of EXODUS should have been called PAIN BONDING 101. By the time I got to EXODUS, surrounded by a bunch of smelly, sweaty slaves, it was pretty obvious the group was doing a lot of bonding over their miserable experiences.

Moses continued, "After Joseph became second in command, his whole family moved to Egypt."

400 YEARS LATER, JACOB'S FAMILY HAD GROWN TO MILLIONS OF PEOPLE, NOW CALLED ISRAELITES. YOU JUST MET SOME OF THEM.

OVER THE YEARS, THE NEW PHARAOHS FORGOT ALL ABOUT WHAT JOSEPH DID AND MADE THE ISRAELITES THEIR SLAVES.

"I'VE ALREADY BEEN IN PRISON WITH JOSEPH!" I yelled. "DO I NEED TO BE A SLAVE, TOO?"

WAH!

"If you think slavery's bad—just wait, it gets worse," Moses yelled back. "This Egyptian Pharaoh is going to command that all the Israelite baby boys be killed just because he hates that there are more Israelites than Egyptians."

Suddenly, WHAP! It hit me. Though I'm not a baby boy and I'm not an Israelite, perhaps a kill-happy nearsighted guard might make a mistake.

KILL THIS ONE NEXT!

DOUBLE OH NO!

That's when I made a strategic decision to stop complaining. I figured the less attention I drew to myself, the better.

Being a slave was one thing. Being dead was quite another.

See Exodus 1:8-22

THURSDAY...

Tonight at dinner Dad told us a GOD STORY from work. For those of you who have never heard of a GOD STORY before, Dad says,

A GOD STORY IS ONE OF THOSE REALLY CRAZY THINGS THAT ONLY MAKE SENSE IF GOD IS INVOLVED.

Somehow Dad has them happen all the time.

DAD'S GOD STORY LIBRARY

ARE YOU SURE YOU AREN'T JUST MAKING THESE UP?

AGE 0-12

AGE 13-19

COLLEGE YEARS

FAMILY/FRIENDS STORIES

CHURCH/WORK STORIES

His most recent story involved a new patient named Don who went to college with Papa Wigglesworth (PW, Dad's dad).

Turns out today when Don had his checkup, he made the connection that he knew Dad's dad in Berkeley, CA, a million zillion years ago.

Don also told Dad that one day after basketball practice, PW gave him his first Bible.

WOW, SO STRANGE MEETING BILL WIGGLESWORTH'S SON IN GASKET, CA.

It's hard to imagine PW ever played basketball. What did he do with his cane?

On my Bible adventure, Moses had his share of GOD stories too. Here's a mind blower.

"Remember Pharaoh's EVIL plan to kill the Israelite baby boys?" Moses said. "I was one of those babies Pharaoh wanted killed. See that mom, girl, and baby over there? Well, they're my MOM, my SISTER, and ME!"

TIME TRAVEL SURE IS COMPLICATED.

Moses continued...

I didn't tell Moses, but I thought it looked like the WORLD'S DUMBEST PLAN. Putting a baby in a basket on the river makes GETTING KILLED even EASIER.

Turned out Moses' mom wasn't totally clueless. She sent his sister Miriam to watch the basket in the river.

It JUST SO HAPPENED that the wicked Pharaoh's daughter came down to the river and found the basket.

And she JUST SO HAPPENED to have baby fever and no MOM skills.

And Miriam JUST SO HAPPENED to tell Pharaoh's daughter she knew an EXPERT mom who could help.

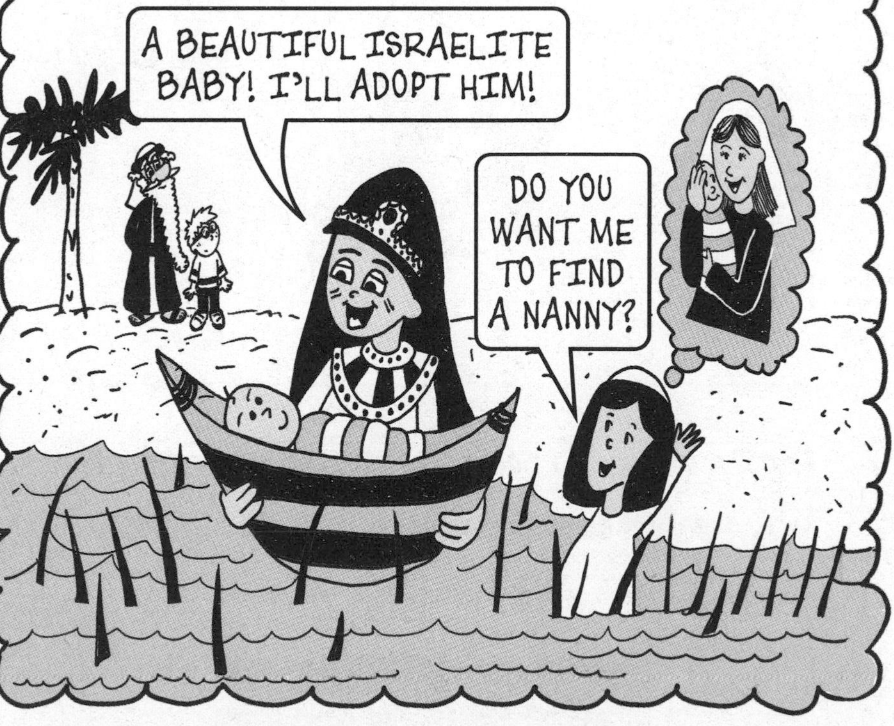
A BEAUTIFUL ISRAELITE BABY! I'LL ADOPT HIM!
DO YOU WANT ME TO FIND A NANNY?

And it JUST SO HAPPENED the daughter's wicked dad, the Pharaoh, had no clue what was going on.

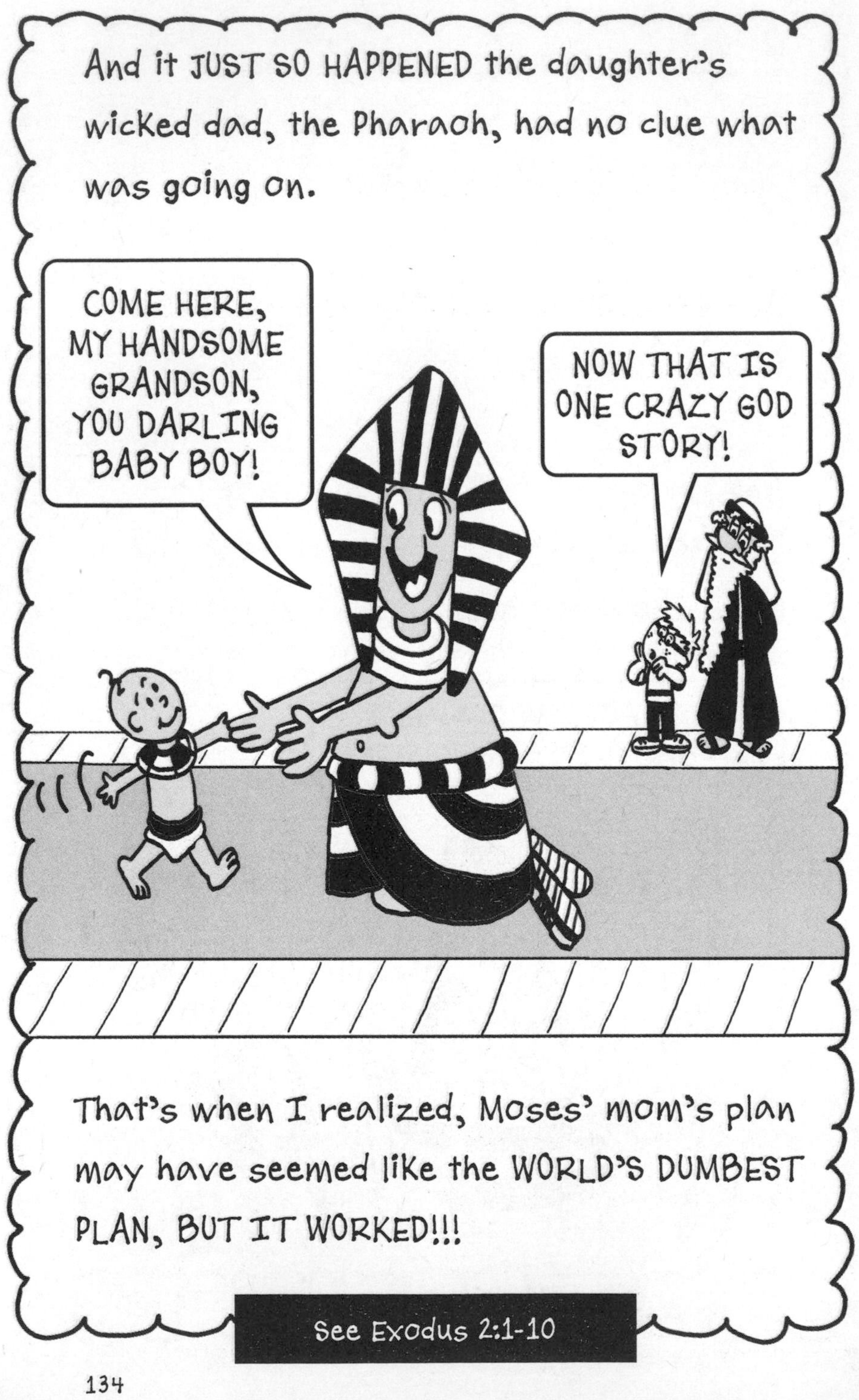
COME HERE, MY HANDSOME GRANDSON, YOU DARLING BABY BOY!
NOW THAT IS ONE CRAZY GOD STORY!

That's when I realized, Moses' mom's plan may have seemed like the WORLD'S DUMBEST PLAN, BUT IT WORKED!!!

See Exodus 2:1-10

MONDAY...

I wish I had an older sister like Miriam who always looked out for her brother Moses rather than a younger sister like Marlee. Marlee tries to do nice things, but it feels like it's really about her.

PATRICK WILL LOVE THIS PICTURE OF ME FOR HIS BIRTHDAY NEXT MONTH!

No offense, Marlee, but even if your intentions are good, I'm over the drama. Especially since the latest episode last Saturday.

My day began wonderfully...

Dad woke me up and said,

PATRICK, YOU'RE BECOMING A MAN, AND A MAN'S BEST FRIEND IS HIS DOG.

IT'S TIME TO GET THAT DOG YOU'VE BEEN BEGGING FOR.

YIPPEE!!! I GET MY VERY OWN DOG!

"But there are two conditions," he continued. "First, it's up to you to feed and walk him DAILY, rain or shine, tired or not!"

"NO PROBLEM!" I responded.

That day Epic entered my life. A 1-year-old male black-and-white something. Straight from the pound.

MY PICK!

You talk about HAPPY! I was over the moon...

...till I found out about the SECOND CONDITION.
Sometimes I had to SHARE Epic with Marlee.

Needless to say, Epic and I no longer felt
manly. If only I could put Marlee in a
basket in a river.

Later, looking Epic in the eye, I knew we were on the same page. No wonder a dog is a man's best friend.

SUNDAY...

Mom said today in Sunday school,

I could have taught that lesson. Especially after my experience with Moses and the burning bush.

You see, even though Moses grew up in Pharaoh's court, he explained to me that when he was 40 years old, he had to flee to the desert because he and Pharaoh had a major falling-out.

It wasn't a quick visit, either. Try 40 years. I arrived in this adventure at the end of Moses' desert time. By then the old Pharaoh had died and a new younger, even meaner Pharaoh had taken over.

PATRICK, WHAT WOULD YOU DO IF YOU HEARD GOD TALKING TO YOU FROM A BURNING BUSH?

HMM...LET ME THINK.

USER-FRIENDLY MANUAL

BIBLE GUIDE TOUR NOTES

Moses barely waited for me to finish sharing my thoughts before he SNAPPED his fingers, and PRESTO, we were in his story standing in front of a REAL burning bush.

Thankfully, I found some mini-binoculars in my right pants pocket, which let me see every detail.

And the search in my pocket worked out doubly well since I also found some fiery red-hot jelly beans.

CLOSE-UP OF ME SPYING AND MUNCHING ON JELLY BEANS.

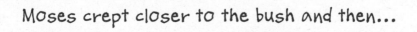

Moses crept closer to the bush and then...

said a deep voice from inside the bush. "This is God! I want you to go to Pharaoh and tell him to LET MY PEOPLE GO!"

If I hadn't been so distracted by the burning bush, I probably could have connected the dots that God wanted Moses to tell Pharaoh to free the Israelite slaves.

But I DIDN'T!

Moses DID, and he wasn't thrilled. So he came up with a bunch of LAME excuses like I do when I want to get out of something.

WHO, ME? I'M JUST A SHEPHERD! WHO WILL BELIEVE THAT YOU SPOKE TO ME? I'M A TERRIBLE PUBLIC SPEAKER!

See Exodus 3

Come to think of it, last summer Billy had his own burning bush story. I never really thought much about it till now.

He said he heard a deep voice speaking from his patio firepit.

Unlike Moses, he didn't question the voice.
"Of course I mowed the lawn all summer,"
he said. "I had no idea Phillip was tricking
me using his SUPERSONIC VOICE CHANGER...
till almost the last day of summer when I
finally woke up."

THE DAY BILLY WOKE UP!!!

WEDNESDAY...

You know how some days you just want to stir things up? Well, today I'm writing a rap about my Bible adventure and Moses' confrontation with Pharaoh.

Mrs. McPherson, who is the queen of corny raps, inspired me. Despite missing the beat half the time, she makes history memorable.

YO, YO, HERE GOES...

WHO SAYS COLUMBUS WAS THE FIRST TO AMERICA IN 1492? WHEN YOU CHECK THE FACTS, YOU'LL FIND IT JUST AIN'T TRUE.

EDGY HISTORY, COOL!

Anyway, you remember Moses standing in front of the burning bush and his lame excuses about why he couldn't speak to Pharaoh. Well, in the end, God told Moses that his brother, Aaron, could come along, and that's when Moses reluctantly agreed to go.

But once we arrived to confront Pharaoh, let's just say Pharaoh was not impressed.

I mean, if glares could kill, we would have gone up in smoke right then. Good thing Aaron was there to take some of the heat and I found 3 pairs of sunglasses in my pocket.

THE GREAT PHARAOH CONFRONTATION RAP

HARD-HEARTED PHARAOH, DON'T YOU KNOW?

GOD WANTS YOU TO LET HIS PEOPLE GO!

NO!

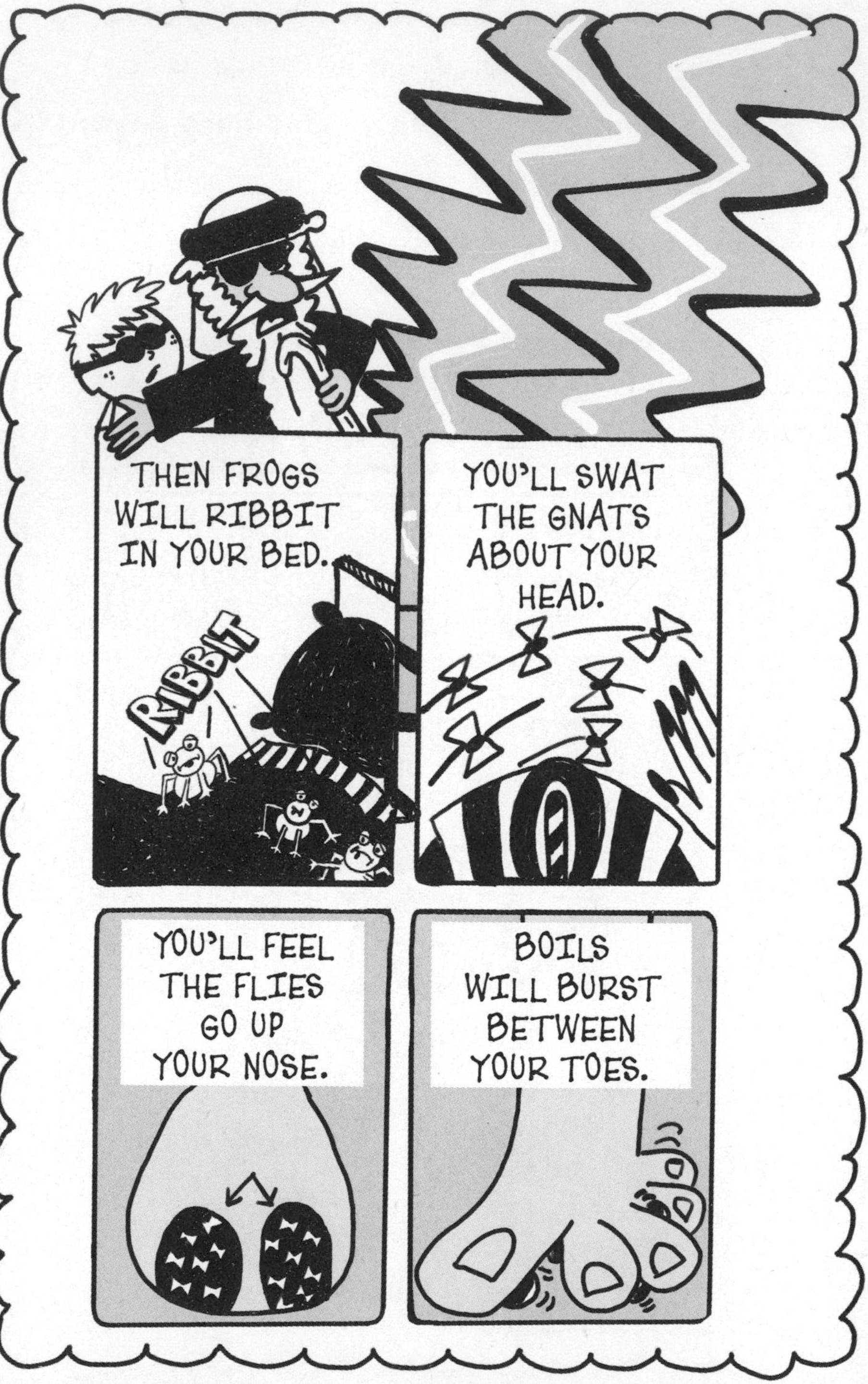
THEN FROGS WILL RIBBIT IN YOUR BED...
RIBBIT
YOU'LL SWAT THE GNATS ABOUT YOUR HEAD.
YOU'LL FEEL THE FLIES GO UP YOUR NOSE.
BOILS WILL BURST BETWEEN YOUR TOES.

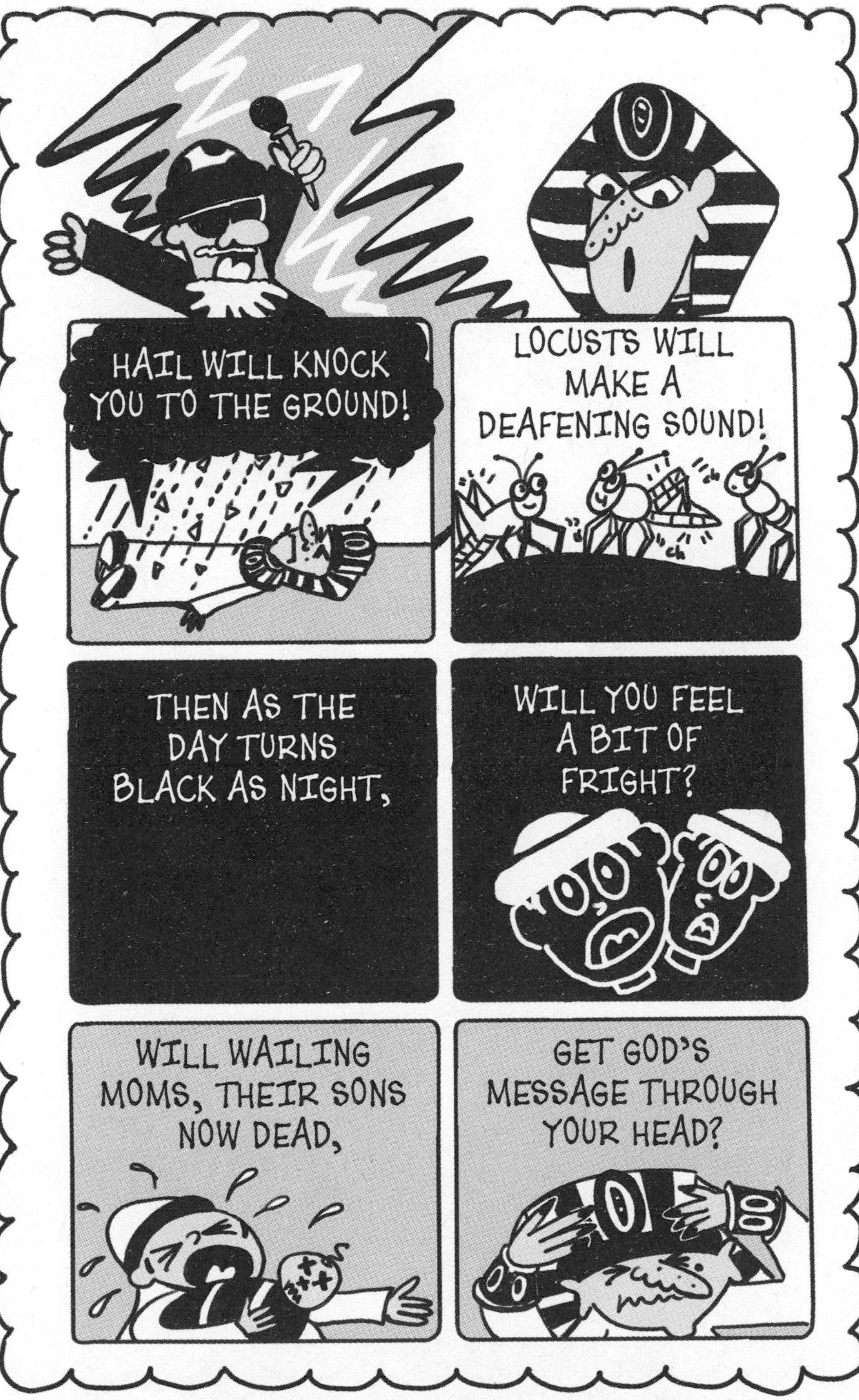
HAIL WILL KNOCK YOU TO THE GROUND!
LOCUSTS WILL MAKE A DEAFENING SOUND!
THEN AS THE DAY TURNS BLACK AS NIGHT,
WILL YOU FEEL A BIT OF FRIGHT?
WILL WAILING MOMS, THEIR SONS NOW DEAD,
GET GOD'S MESSAGE THROUGH YOUR HEAD?

Finally Pharaoh had enough, so he sent the Israelites packing—and we HIGHTAILED IT OUT OF THERE.

TALK ABOUT SOMEONE BEING A SORE LOSER.

See Exodus 5:1—12:32

FRIDAY...

I HATE packing! WAY too many DECISIONS.
Mom says we are going to Nana and PW's
house for the weekend.

PATRICK,
WANT TO
SHARE A
SUITCASE
WITH ME?

UMM,
I'LL
PASS!

Some say I look like my Nana. Me? I don't
see the resemblance.

Resemblance or not, a weekend with Nana
and PW has lots of PERKS!

Especially PW's leaning tower of pancakes.

Then all-day board games, and more food.

Too bad PW's asleep by 7:00 P.M.

I STILL THINK IT'S WEIRD HE GOES TO SLEEP THE SAME TIME I DID IN KINDERGARTEN.

But, for now, I've got my work cut out for me deciding what to PACK.

I'm glad I didn't have to pack ANYTHING the day Pharaoh told the Israelites, "GO!" It was a MADHOUSE and it was hard enough just to stay out of the way.

Imagine millions of people, living in the same place for 400 years, sorting through 5 billion zillion tons of stuff to figure out what they could carry or put on a rickety cart.

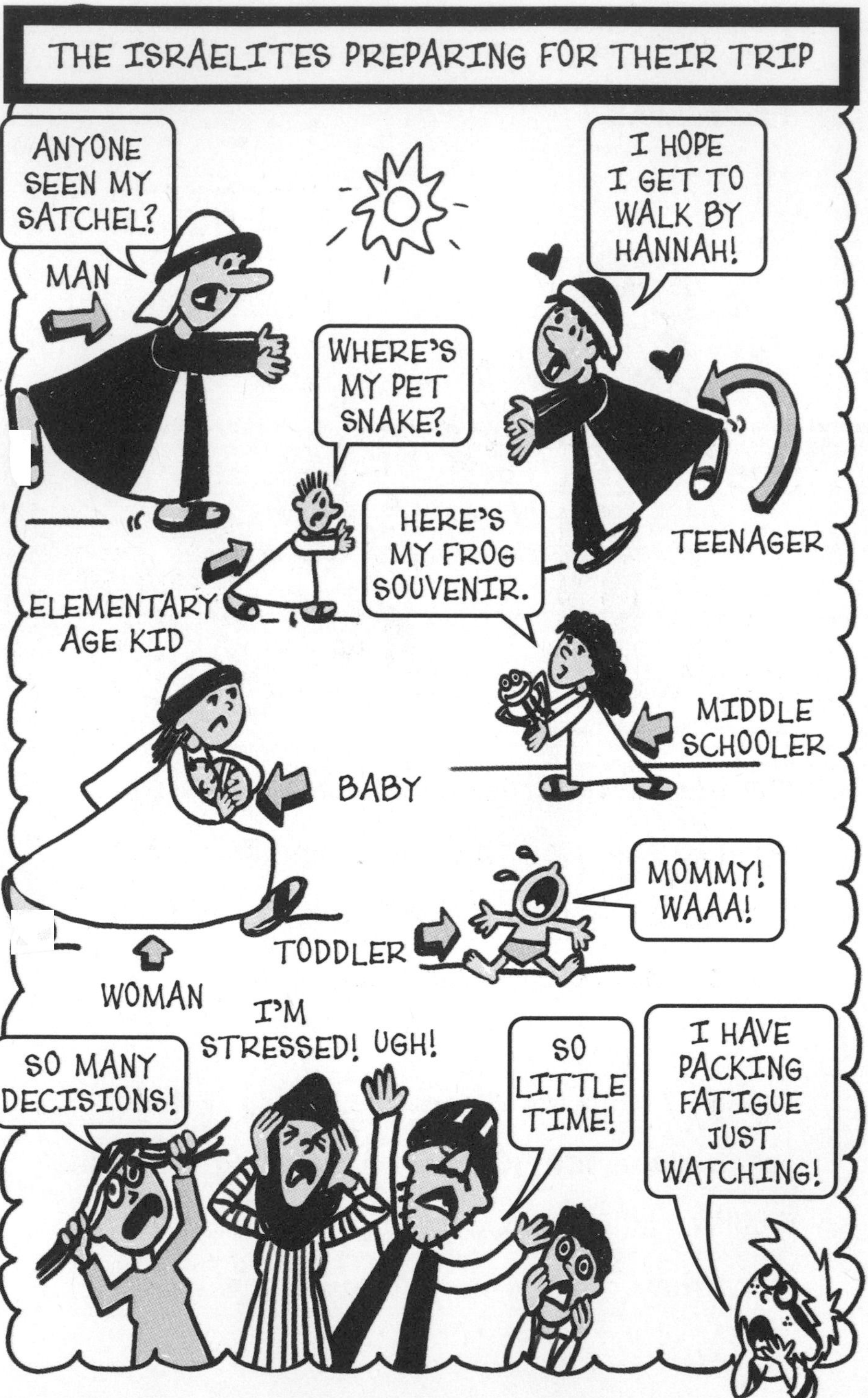
THE ISRAELITES PREPARING FOR THEIR TRIP
ANYONE SEEN MY SATCHEL?
MAN
I HOPE I GET TO WALK BY HANNAH!
WHERE'S MY PET SNAKE?
HERE'S MY FROG SOUVENIR.
TEENAGER
ELEMENTARY AGE KID
MIDDLE SCHOOLER
BABY
MOMMY! WAAA!
TODDLER
WOMAN
I'M STRESSED! UGH!
SO MANY DECISIONS!
SO LITTLE TIME!
I HAVE PACKING FATIGUE JUST WATCHING!

To make matters worse, God told Pharaoh's people, the Egyptians, to give the Israelites ALL their BIG TICKET items.

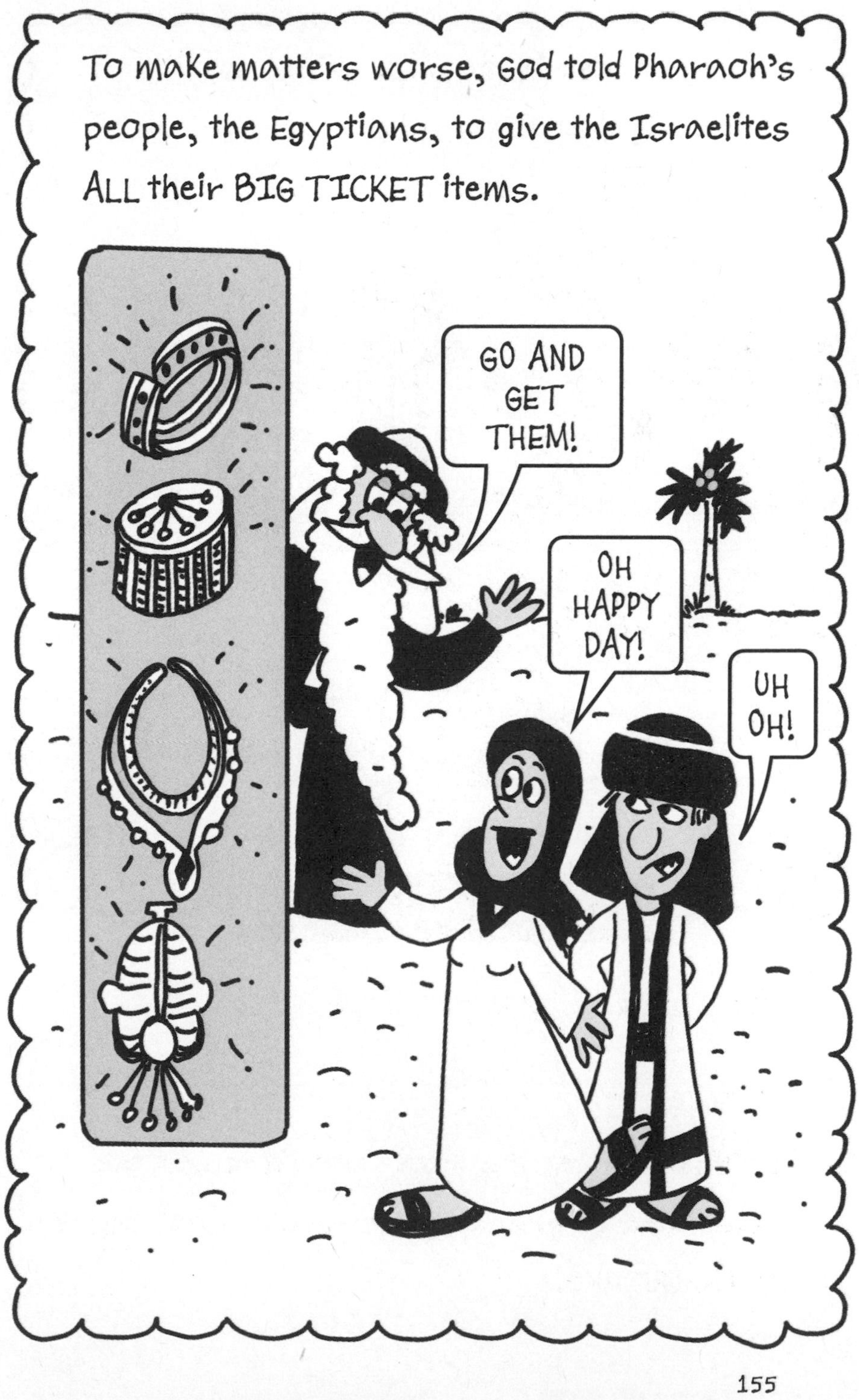
GO AND GET THEM!
OH HAPPY DAY!
UH OH!

Like I said, I hate packing.

SUNDAY...

I think you get the idea that PW is not the usual kind of grandpa. Here are a few more of his QUIRKS.

First, he flosses his teeth every hour on the hour, and he keeps his floss wrapped around his cane.

Second, if you EAT PW's famous pancakes, you are required to go on one of his 5-mile post breakfast "hikes." It's actually more like a jog with PW's cane leading the way.

Unfortunately, today while hiking I watched his QUIRKINESS reach a whole new level.

Take, for example, how he used his cane to push aside tree limbs and bushes, double-contaminating his floss.

Then he unraveled the floss and plunked it between his teeth, not giving any thought to the possibility of getting POISON OAK IN HIS MOUTH.

RISKY, right?

Although maybe I shouldn't be too judgmental because on my Bible adventure desert hike I had my own weird mouth experience.

After Pharaoh told us to GO, and everyone was done packing, we began walking in the desert. I just followed along till finally I had to ask the obvious question.

BY THE WAY, MOSES, WHERE ARE WE GOING?

WHEREVER THAT PILLAR OF CLOUD LEADS US.

Talk about an unsatisfactory answer! Since I had never followed a cloud before and I'm BIG on knowing my destination, I pestered Moses for more details.

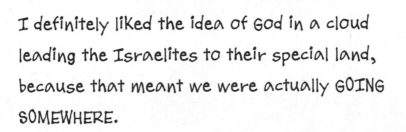

BUT WHY FOLLOW THAT CLOUD?

BECAUSE GOD IS IN THAT CLOUD, LEADING US TO A SPECIAL LAND HE PROMISED US.

I definitely liked the idea of God in a cloud leading the Israelites to their special land, because that meant we were actually GOING SOMEWHERE.

But it wasn't long before I had another PROBLEM!

Not to be irreverent, but as we trudged along in the dry desert, that God-filled towering white cloud got me thinking about cotton candy. Which reminded me how much I  cotton candy. Which made my mouth drool.

Not just a few drops of drool, but GUSHING drool that sprayed EVERYWHERE.

The kid behind me DID NOT appreciate my dilemma.

SORRY, BUT IF YOU KNEW WHAT COTTON CANDY TASTED LIKE, YOU'D BE DROOLING TOO.

Then suddenly my problem resolved itself. We came to the RED SEA, and the cloud stopped moving. And once it stopped moving, it no longer looked fluffy like cotton candy.

My mirage changed. It now reminded me of a clump of marshmallows.

PROBLEM SOLVED! Marshmallows make me

SICK!!!

Thank you, God, for Cub Scout camp and 12 S'MORES!

See Exodus 13:17-22

163

WEDNESDAY...

Every day Derrick takes the same route home from school like clockwork.

UNTIL TODAY!

Probably something to do with an update to his Nasty Newton Checklist!

DAILY NASTIES

☒ KICK DOG

☒ PULL CAT'S TAIL

☒ TIP OVER A GARBAGE CAN

TODAY'S UPDATE

☐ CHANGE ROUTE HOME TO PUNISH PATRICK FOR MAKING ME LOOK BAD IN THE MAMBA JUICE POSTER CONTEST.

That's when my perfectly planned Avoid-Derrick-at-Any-Cost route home went down the tubes.

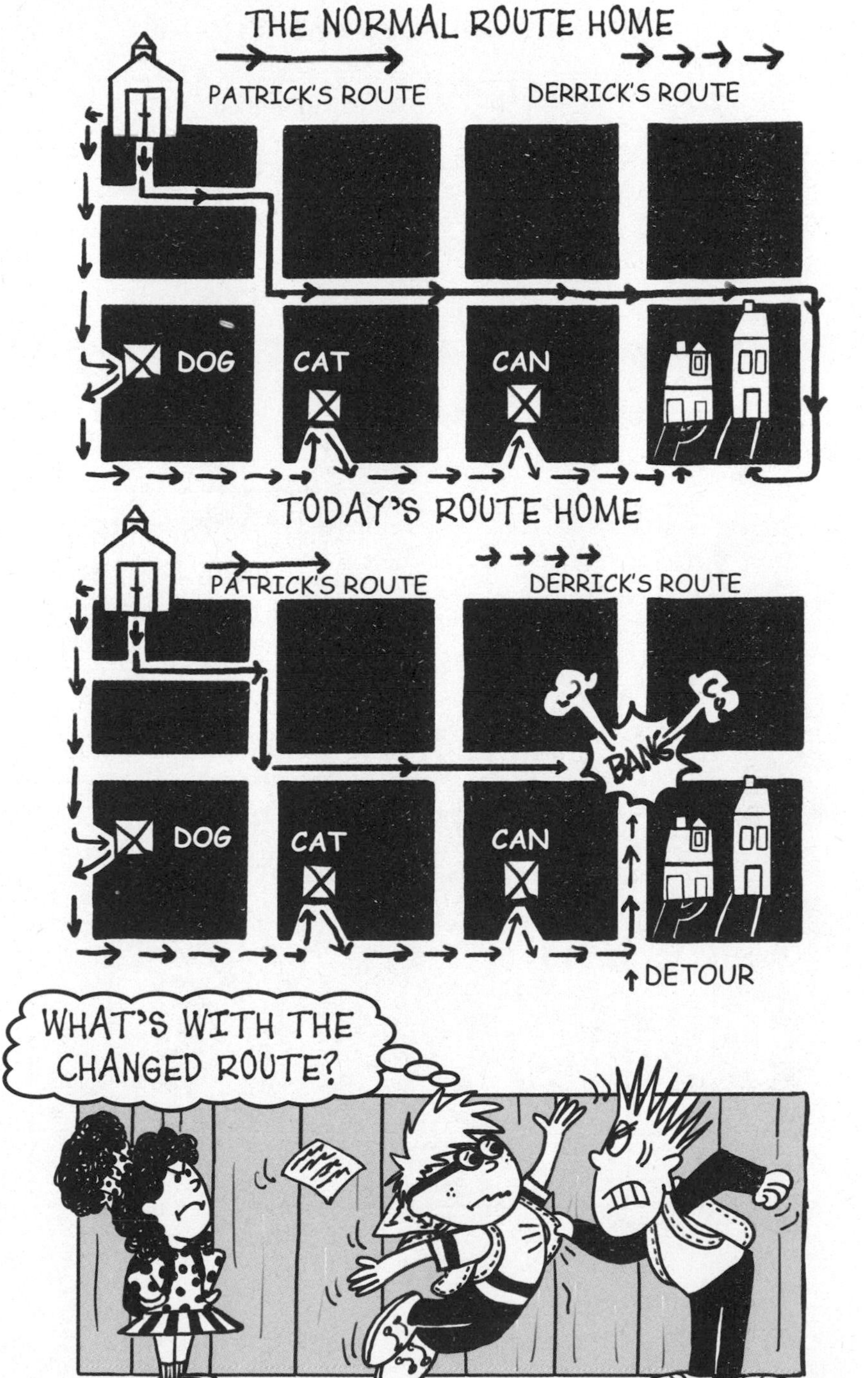

THE NORMAL ROUTE HOME
PATRICK'S ROUTE
DERRICK'S ROUTE
DOG
CAT
CAN
TODAY'S ROUTE HOME
PATRICK'S ROUTE
DERRICK'S ROUTE
BANG
DOG
CAT
CAN
DETOUR
WHAT'S WITH THE CHANGED ROUTE?

Lucky for me, Mrs. Smelly, Gasket's chief busybody and head of the GARDEN SOCIETY, chose that moment to pop her head over the fence.

Derrick, caught red-handed, put on his innocent face and chatted her up.

WHY, MRS. SMELLY, YOU HAVE THE MOST BEAUTIFUL ROSES! COULD YOU TELL ME HOW THEY GROW SO BIG?

Marlee took advantage of the distraction.

Doubling my humiliation!

FRIDAY...

I think I should pat myself on the back because I'm not flaking out on writing my Bible adventure. Even Epic's proud of me. His wagging tail says it all...

ONLY 5 MORE MINUTES TILL MY WALK!!!

Pharaoh, on the other hand, was off the charts in flakiness. Remember how he commanded the Israelites to stay in Egypt, then he told them to go? Well, now he had ANOTHER thought.

I'VE CHANGED MY MIND. BRING THEM BACK!

I guess his mother never taught him... LET YOUR YES BE YES AND YOUR NO BE NO!

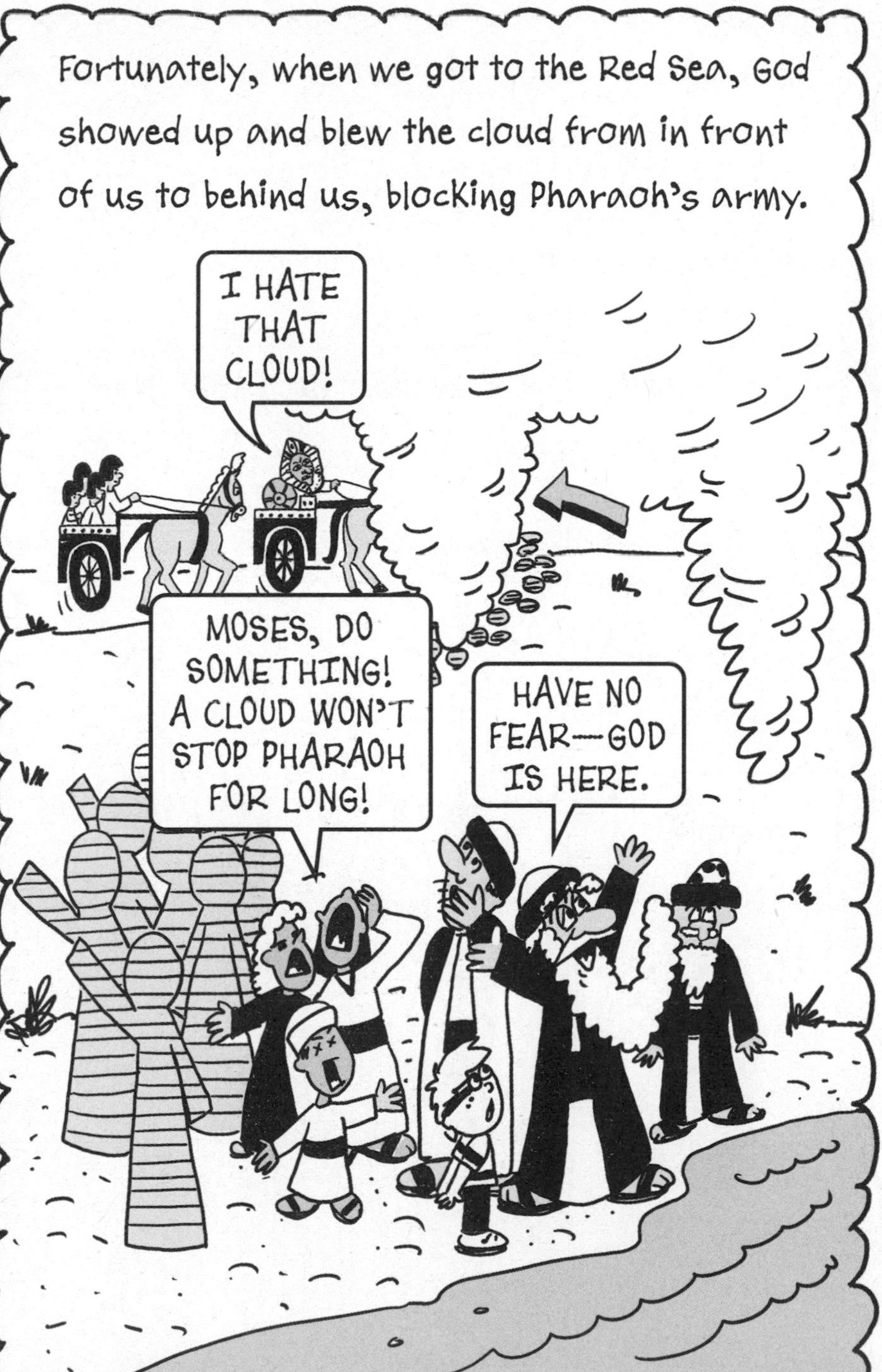
Fortunately, when we got to the Red Sea, God showed up and blew the cloud from in front of us to behind us, blocking Pharaoh's army.
I HATE THAT CLOUD!
MOSES, DO SOMETHING! A CLOUD WON'T STOP PHARAOH FOR LONG!
HAVE NO FEAR—GOD IS HERE.

Then God made a fierce wind divide the sea into two gigantic standing waves with a TOTALLY dry path right down the middle. Moses led all of us down that path.

I felt bad for the fish that got separated from their families.

Thinking about it now, I probably understood the whole fish staring at you from behind a wall of water phenomenon way better than the Israelites as I've visited the Monterey Bay Aquarium a bunch of times.

Of course, without the glass between you and the water, it's much more fun. Check out my finger wake.

DAD, WHAT'S HE DOING? CAN I DO THAT TOO?

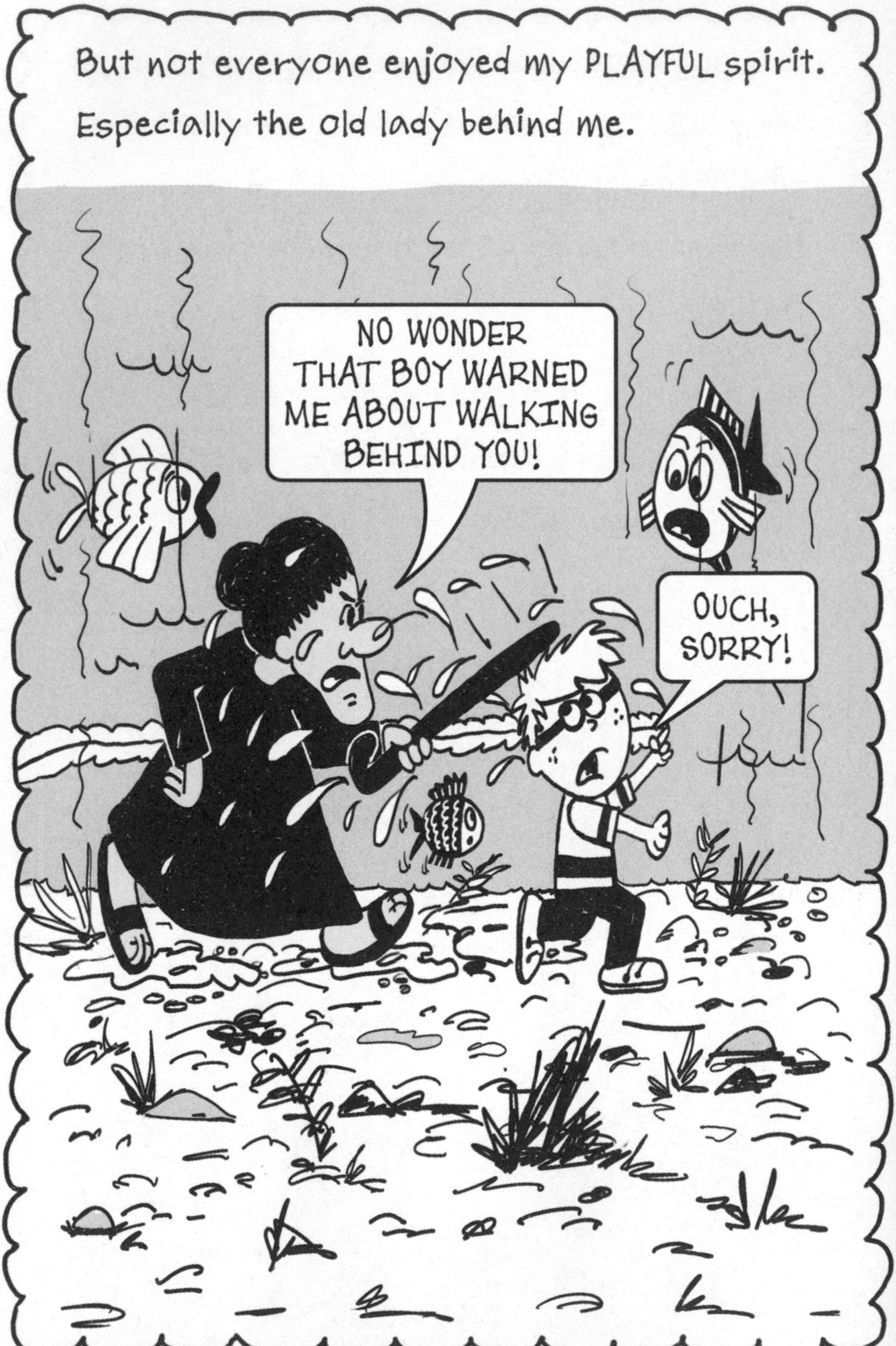
But not everyone enjoyed my PLAYFUL spirit.
Especially the old lady behind me.
NO WONDER THAT BOY WARNED ME ABOUT WALKING BEHIND YOU!
OUCH, SORRY!

Still not sure why she gave me such a hard time. I did her a HUGE FAVOR. Mom pays big bucks at Betty's Beauty School to have stuff splashed all over her face. And that lady needed it much more than Mom.

By the way, it's amazing what the bottom of a sea looks like without water. Slimy rocks, ferny plants, and SUNKEN TREASURE. I kept thinking the whole time, "Too bad I don't have Dad's metal detector. I could be raking it in."

A-HUNTING I WILL GO,
A-HUNTING I WILL GO,
HEIGH HO, THE DERRY-O,
A-HUNTING I WILL GO!

However, when God turned off the wind, watching Pharaoh's army get swallowed up by the sea cured me of ever wanting to see the ocean's bottom again.

THANK YOU, GOD, FOR SAVING US FROM PHARAOH!

See Exodus 14:1—15:21

TUESDAY...

Today in health class, Mrs. McPherson told us we should drink 6 glasses of water a day. Mom says 7. Nana says, "Do what your mom says!"

Mom is REALLY serious about this. She even puts out 7 bowls of water for Epic. Epic doesn't mind—it's his one daily choice.

EENY, MEENY, MINY, MOE...

#1 #2
#3 #4
#5 #6 #7

I make it easy. No counting glasses, just one drinking fountain trip during each of my 7 classes.

THIS IS AN ALMOST PERFECT SYSTEM EXCEPT I'M ABOUT TO FLOAT AWAY.

On my Bible adventure in the desert, there were NO debates about how much water to drink. We were happy if we got ANY.

I remember the day God told Moses to STRIKE a rock with his staff to create a crazy cool drinking fountain.

With one fountain and millions of thirsty folks, you had to think of ways to pass the time while standing in line.

The line seemed to go on forever.

After a few rounds of standing in line, being from the future came in handy. Gotta love those plastic water bottles I found in my pocket. Thank you, Bible adventure right pants pocket, for again providing everything I needed.

See Exodus 17:1-7

FRIDAY...

This weekend Mom says we are going camping because we need more

FUN FAMILY TIME!

Why do we need more FAMILY TIME? We see each other 7 days a week. Besides, 4 people plus Epic stacked on top of each other in a tiny tent is hardly FUN.

Mom tried to motivate us to enjoy camping.

REALLY, MOM! On my Bible adventure I saw that tent and it was NOTHING like this CAMPMART special.

FIRST OFF, it had a NAME. THE TABERNACLE!

The only name I'd give our tent is CHEAP.

SECOND, it was CUSTOM DESIGNED. God gave

Moses specific instructions...

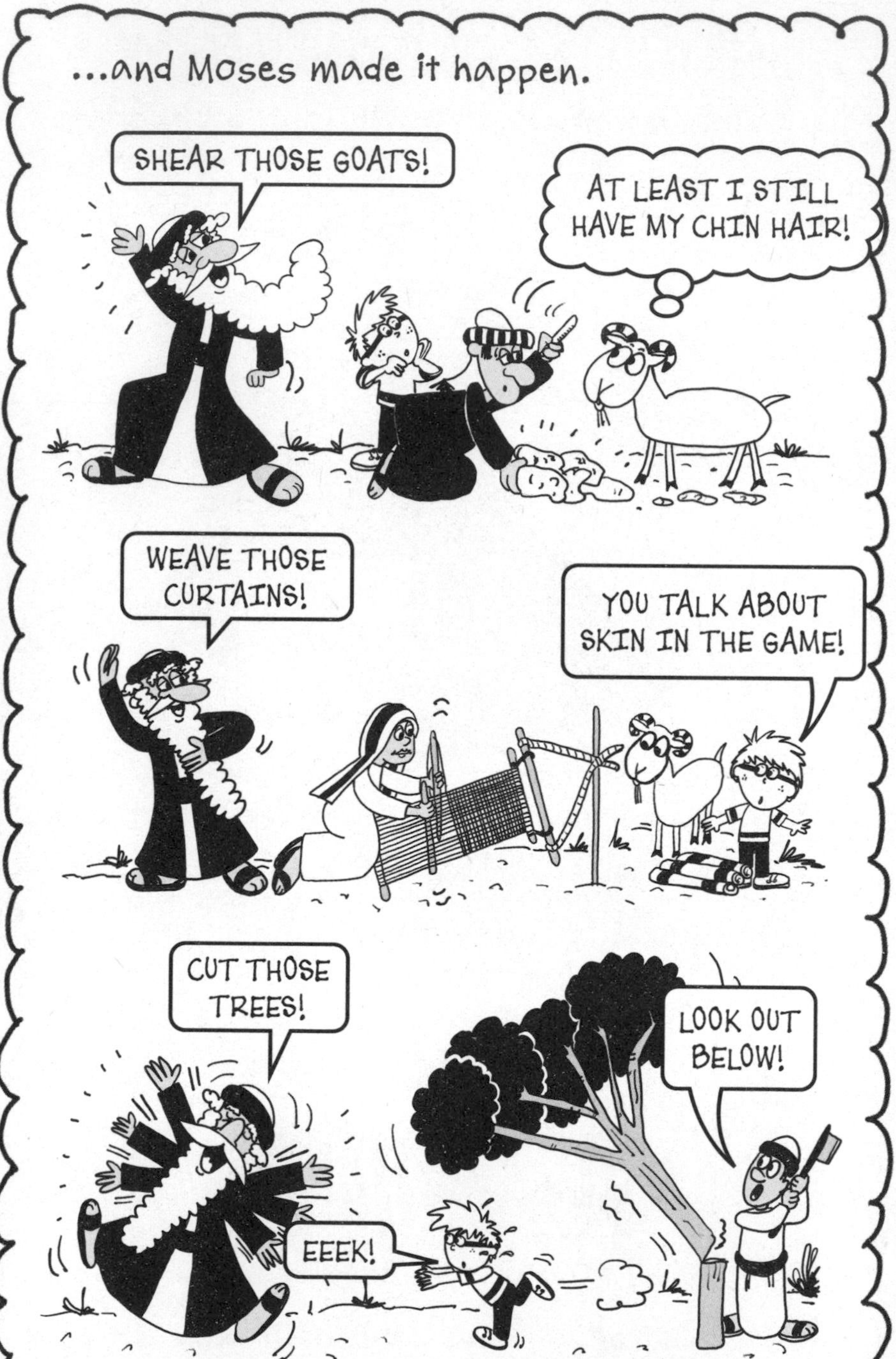
...and Moses made it happen.
SHEAR THOSE GOATS!
AT LEAST I STILL HAVE MY CHIN HAIR!
WEAVE THOSE CURTAINS!
YOU TALK ABOUT SKIN IN THE GAME!
CUT THOSE TREES!
LOOK OUT BELOW!
EEEK!

THIRD, it was MASSIVE! With a bath and incense altar in the courtyard.

GOD WAS IN THE CLOUD THAT COVERED THE TENT.

BATH

ALTAR

See Exodus 26, 27, 36—38, 40

OK, Mom—yes, God CAMPED with the Israelites. But if you really want to motivate ME...

WE NEED A BIGGER, BETTER TENT.

SATURDAY...

I'm hiding out in my tree fort with my journal and Epic. Hoisting Epic up here in my backpack is always tricky, but worth it.

Every time I finish recording a new day in my journal, I read it to Epic. He's so encouraging. After I shared my most recent entries, he wagged his tail 7 times at the part where he picked his water dish.

He's going to love this next entry too. After all, he has a lot in common with the Israelites waiting while Moses went up the mountain to visit God.

Us waiting at the bottom of Mount Sinai.

Epic waiting at the bottom of my tree fort.

THE ISRAELITES

He's also going to relate to how excited Moses got whenever he hiked up Mount Sinai to see God. I'll bet Epic feels the same way when I pull him up to see me.

Here's the rest of that Bible adventure.
I hope you like it, Epic.

After Moses went up the mountain, I couldn't believe how fast the Israelites adopted the motto "Out of sight, out of mind." Immediately they forgot all about God and melted down their Egyptian jewelry to make a statue to worship.

OH BEAUTIFUL GOLDEN COW, WE WORSHIP YOU!

I'LL JUST READ THIS COMIC BOOK!

As you can imagine, when Moses came back down from the mountain 40 days later, carrying God's 10 Commandments, he was NOT HAPPY!

In fact, the 2 carved stone tablets got the brunt of his anger.

I don't think they'll EVER forget what Moses taught them next.

He made the Israelites grind up their golden calf and put it in their water!

I GUESS THE LESSON IS—DON'T WORSHIP SOMETHING YOU CAN DRINK!

WHAT!

MANDATORY!

GOLDEN CALF SODA

You think braces sparkle. Gold dust has that BEAT.

And while Moses hiked back up Mount Sinai for two more stone tablets, I'm glad to report that no one messed around the whole time he was gone. Besides, they were busy picking gold out of their teeth.

DID I GET IT ALL?

See Exodus 32, 34

EPIC, YOU'D NEVER MESS AROUND IF I WAS GONE FOR A WHILE, WOULD YOU?

THURSDAY...

My journey out of EXODUS into the next Bible book was a LITTLE ROUGH. Moses carefully pronounced the name of the book.

LE-VI-TI-CUS!

SOUNDS LIKE A "CUSS" WORD TO ME!

But who was I to question the name of a Bible book?

Especially since my bone-jarring landing in LE-VI-TI-CUS left my brain buzzing. I felt like a text that someone just sent. Moses called it "BOOK-LAG."

Moses said visiting this book would be quick.
It didn't matter much to me because once
my brain calmed down, LEVITICUS looked a
lot like EXODUS. Sun, bugs, desert, and the
Israelites, till Moses said...

Then Moses dragged me over to meet some guys called priests. He said, "They teach the Israelites to follow God's rules."

Thinking about it now, I don't envy the priests' job. Just last week I tried to teach Epic where to do his business. That one rule about destroyed our friendship.

Anyway, I did think the priests' outfits were pretty cool lookin'.

ARE YOU A COOK ON THE SIDE?

I especially liked their job initiation ceremony where they were drenched with oil.

OOH, COUNT ME IN!

See Leviticus 8:30, 10:10-11

Recently, I've been thinking about starting my own club with an initiation and everything.

Although my initiation will not just involve oil but also a razor.

I think the best thing about starting your own club is you get to make up YOUR OWN rules.

Like...

1. Derrick Newton will NEVER be a member.
2. Derrick Newton will NEVER EVER be a member.
3. Derrick Newton will NEVER EVER, EVER, EVER, EVER be a member.

That feels like a pretty good start.

SATURDAY...

TODAY'S MY BIRTHDAY! Birthdays are a BIG
DEAL in our house despite my parents' TIGHT
budget. They say living on a budget lets them
give away more money to charities.

I think I'M a pretty good charity. Just give
it to ME.

Dad also says, "Birthday parties can be
BUDGET BUSTERS."

But Mom's found a way for him to save
on gas to fund my party.

HONEY, IT'S THAT TIME OF YEAR AGAIN. HERE'S YOUR BUS PASS!

Patrick's BIRTHDAY MONTH

ANYTHING FOR THE BUDGET AND PATRICK'S BDAY!

Thanks to Dad, my friends and I were off
to the WILD WATER PARK.

WAIT UP FOR THE BIRTHDAY BOY!

One thing about the WILD WATER PARK—
they have LOTS of rules.

NO

RUNNING
DIVING
EATING
DUNKING
PUSHING
SHOVING

HAVE...
FUN!

The WILD WATER PARK owners and God must be on the same wavelength.

In LEVITICUS, when God told the Israelites to throw a bunch of feasts, he even included party rules.

CHECK OUT GOD'S PARTY RULES INVOLVING BREAD.

FEAST OF UNLEAVENED BREAD RULES:
1. START PARTY ON THE 15TH DAY OF THE MONTH.

2. PARTY FOR 7 DAYS.

3. EAT ONLY UNLEAVENED BREAD FOR THOSE 7 DAYS. (UNLEAVENED BREAD IS A SPECIAL BREAD THAT'S REALLY FLAT.)

DOES SOURDOUGH BREAD GET A PARTY TOO?

See Leviticus 23:4-8

In my opinion, rules take the FUN out of
parties. So I asked my parents...

Much to my surprise, Mom said OK, too.

"Patrick, TODAY'S YOUR NO-RULES BIRTHDAY,"
she exclaimed while carrying a CHUNKY
CHOCOLATE THREE-LAYER BIRTHDAY CAKE
from BETTY'S BAKERY in from the kitchen.

Naturally, I... *went for it!*

I SPIT ON MY CAKE AS I BLEW OUT THE CANDLES,

TALKED WITH MY MOUTH FULL, ATE WITH MY HANDS, AND HOGGED ALL THE FOOD.

Everything was perfect till I finished off the second layer of the cake.

Which made me reconsider. Maybe a rule or two for parties wouldn't be the end of the world.

SUNDAY...

After church today, Billy and I went over to Simon's house.

What kid does that? We found out later, Simon had been busy writing the numbers from 1 to a MILLION till his hand cramped.

Most people would call him COUNTING obsessed. Not me! When you have a brainiac math whiz inventor as a best friend, it comes with the territory.

Besides, God's totally into COUNTING!

DID YOU KNOW GOD COUNTS EVERY HAIR ON YOUR HEAD?

DO NOSE HAIRS COUNT?!

When I arrived in the book of Numbers on my Bible adventure, I heard God tell Moses to count every male age 20 or older in each of the 12 tribes of the Israelites.

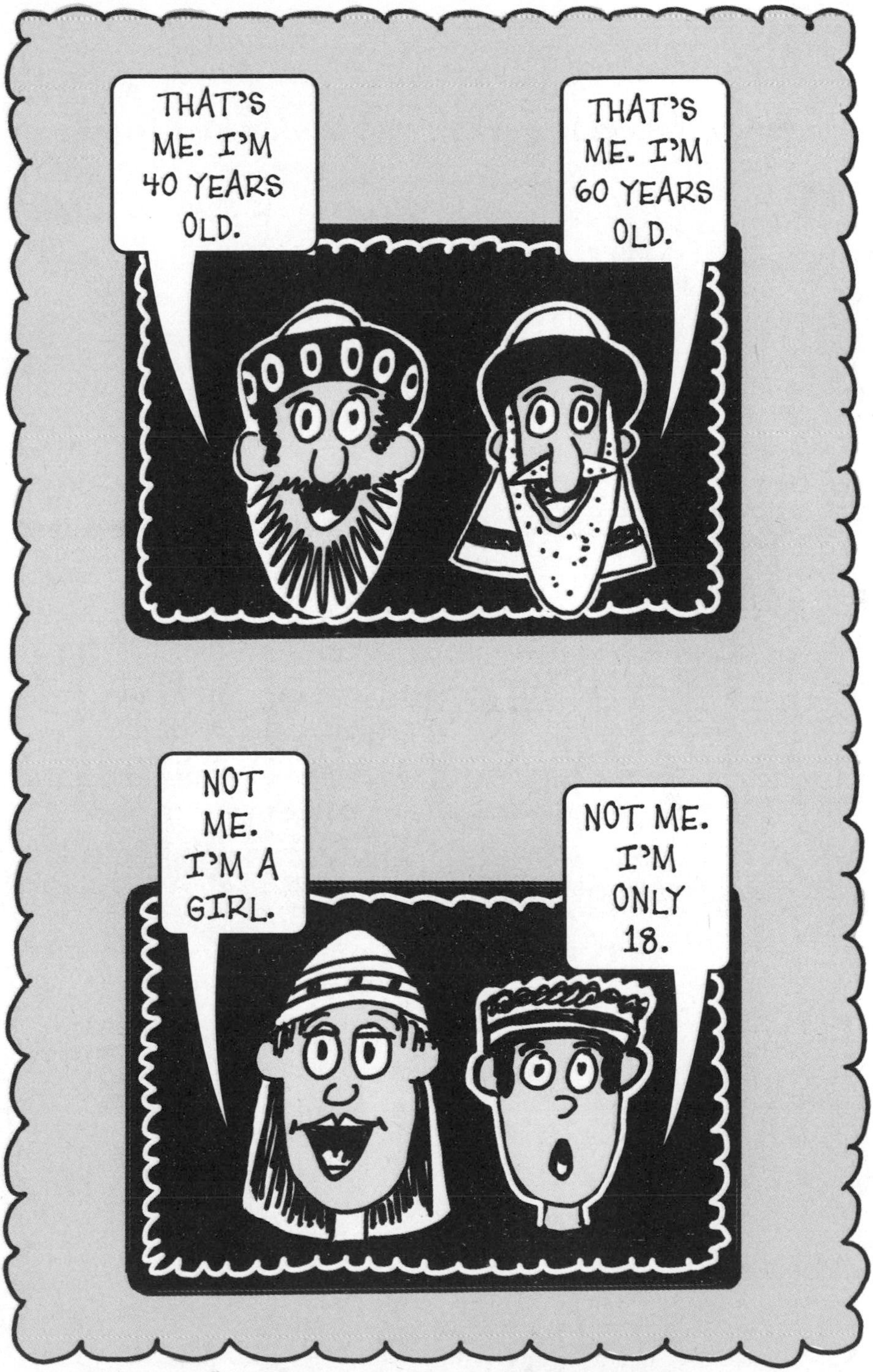
THAT'S ME. I'M 40 YEARS OLD.
THAT'S ME. I'M 60 YEARS OLD.
NOT ME. I'M A GIRL.
NOT ME. I'M ONLY 18.

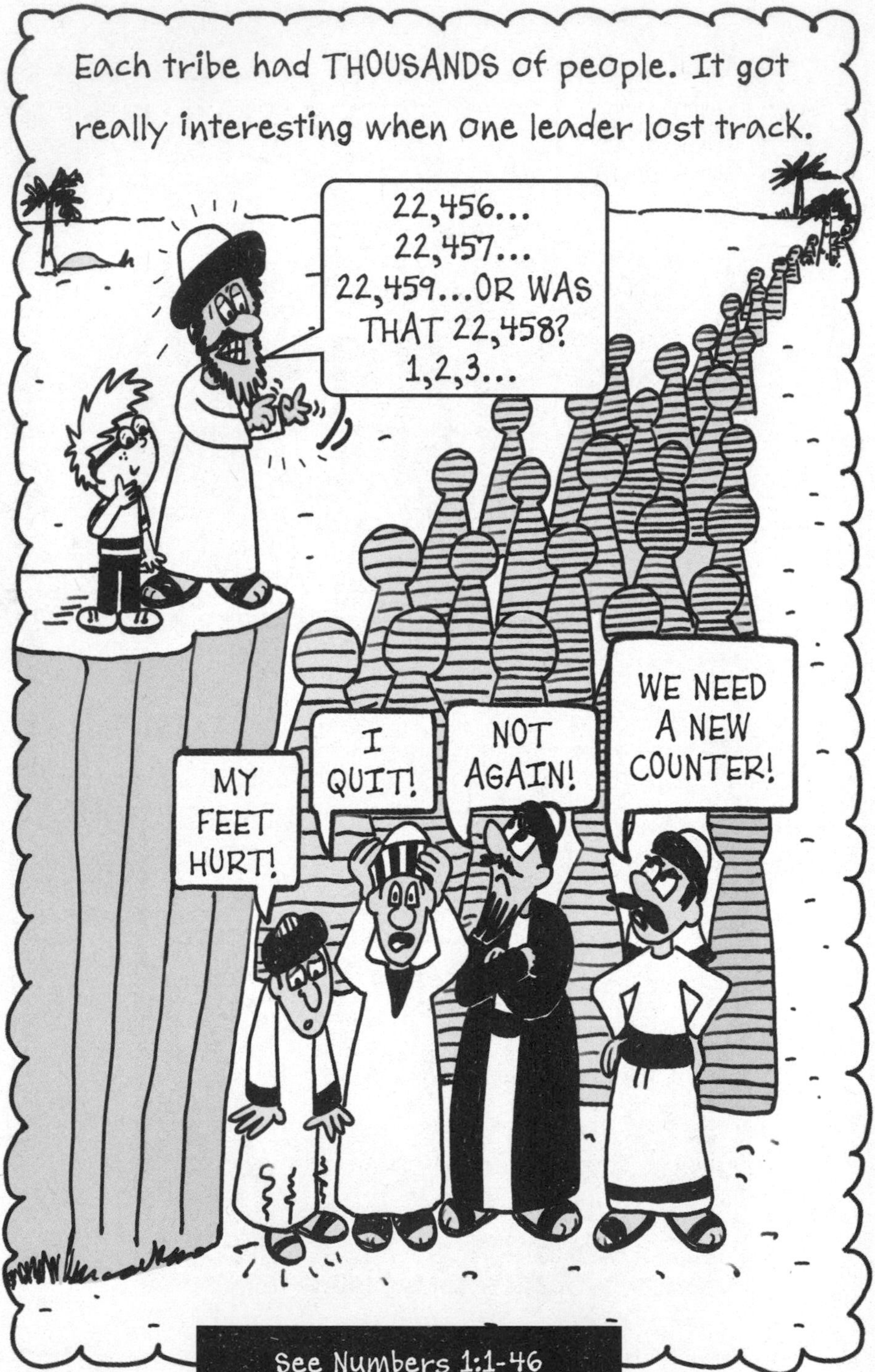
Each tribe had THOUSANDS of people. It got really interesting when one leader lost track.
22,456...
22,457...
22,459...OR WAS THAT 22,458?
1,2,3...
MY FEET HURT!
I QUIT!
NOT AGAIN!
WE NEED A NEW COUNTER!
See Numbers 1:1-46

THURSDAY...

I'm definitely a BIG PICTURE thinker, someone who sees great ideas and figures out how to market them.

Simon and I make a perfect duo. When he comes up with that REALLY AWESOME invention, I'm his guy.

Till then, I've always got my eyes open. That's why I was so stoked on my Bible adventure by GOD's AMAZING desert food called MANNA!

Although the name didn't have much POP, that honey-flavored treat literally melted in my mouth. Which sent my brain buzzing with great MARKETING ONE-LINERS.

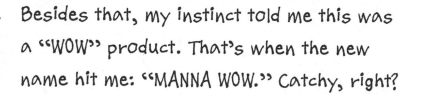

LOVE AT FIRST BITE!

MAGICAL MINI-WAFERS!

DELICIOUS DESERT DELICACIES!

Besides that, my instinct told me this was a "WOW" product. That's when the new name hit me: "MANNA WOW." Catchy, right?

Health-minded moms like mine would have loved MANNA'S "I never get sick" testimonials by the Israelites.

Here was my GENIUS plan. If I could just get the exclusive licensing rights, I'd corner the market and make millions.

Not that I'm greedy or anything. I even had a plan for sharing with Good Shepherd Church.

Forget a 10% tithe, I would give 50%! Possibly 60% depending on my margins.

But I had one major PROBLEM. I DIDN'T have the RECIPE. Manna just appeared every morning...

and disappeared every night.

GOODBYE, MANNA!

That didn't leave me much time to reverse engineer the ingredients. Although I did try...

MAYBE THERE'S 1/2 T. HONEY—NO, 1/4 T. HOW ABOUT...

PATRICK, LET'S GO!

Then another bright idea hit me. I knew Moses had BIG connections with God. I could cut him in on the deal.

IF YOU GET THE RECIPE FOR MANNA, I'LL SIGN A NONDISCLOSURE AGREEMENT AND PROMISE YOU A 20% CUT. WHAT DO YOU THINK?

WHO IS THIS KID?

Unfortunately, I could never get Moses to bite. Maybe he didn't understand my MASSIVE consumer audience. Especially how the "grab and go" food concept is BIG MONEY!

MANNA WOW

MANNA WOW!

Manna...
Smoothies
Burritos
Crepes
Chips
Popcorn
...kies

SORRY, I DON'T CARRY CHANGE, BUT TIPS ARE WELCOME!

See Exodus 16; Numbers 11:7-9

214

Notes to self about marketing great products like MANNA WOW:

I'm thinking now it's probably best to focus on my OWN product line, this BIZARRE BIBLE ADVENTURE series I'm writing. After all, there are no partners to convince, and I own ALL the rights.

Besides, I'm feeling pretty confident about its success. It must be a great idea because

YOU'RE STILL READING IT!

TUESDAY...

I like to complain just as much as the next kid, but when we complain at our house, something BAD always happens.

Take dinner tonight. I started complaining about the lima beans. What self-respecting kid doesn't hate lima beans?

Mom didn't say a word. She just picked up my plate, dividing ALL my food onto everyone else's plates. That shut me up FAST!

216

Unlike me, some people seem to get off SCOT-FREE when they complain. Take the Israelites, for example. Most of them were CHAMPION complainers.

But, instead of taking away their dinner like Mom always does, God blew in a bunch of quail for them to eat.

I felt sorry for those quail. The more time I spent listening to them, the more sympathy I had.

I CAN SEE WHY YOU WOULD BE UPSET!

After all, I wouldn't want to be turned into a dinner menu item.

ISRAELITE DINNER *MENU*

QUAIL BURGER

QUAIL DOG

QUAIL PIZZA

Anyway, I shouldn't have worried that the greedy Israelites would get off SCOT-FREE.

See Numbers 11:4-6, 31-34

I'm still not sure why the Israelites put up such a fuss about eating MANNA. I love the stuff.

Now, if it had been lima beans for 40 years... I would have understood.

SATURDAY...

Mrs. McPherson is partnering me and Derrick Newton on the end-of-year science project. WHAT is she THINKING? Doesn't she know Derrick's my ARCHENEMY?

I could tell something was up when Derrick began to turn his "Teacher's Suck-Up" charm onto me.

Then after Derrick finished talking, VOILA, he reached under his desk and pulled out a box.

Mrs. McPherson was very impressed by Derrick's enthusiasm, but she went on to tell us that although we were a team, we each had to do separate work and would be graded individually.

I just kept thinking, OK, all I have to do is copy Derrick's model, put the rain gauge in my backyard, check it every 24 hours for 7 days, and note the level of rainfall. Total no-brainer, RIGHT?

But still, my supersonic rat sensor sounded its alarm.

In the end, Mrs. McPherson's beaming smile OVERRULED. As the first team with a decent idea, I could tell we made her day.

And since a happy teacher usually makes for happy students, I decided to go along with Derrick's experiment.

Too bad EVERYTHING went DOWNHILL from there.

DAY 1: No rain but my rain gauge overflowed...

DAY 2: Lots of rain but my rain gauge was empty...

7 days of crazy numbers for me. Not even close to the OFFICIAL Gasket rain data.

NOTE TO SELF: Don't ignore my built-in supersonic rat sensor. If it smells a rat, set a trap.

SUNDAY...

Even though my foolish decision to trust Derrick caused me to fail my science project, it was not as bad as the foolish decision I saw the Israelites make when they trusted some of their FRIENDS. Here's how that went down.

We'd been traveling in the desert for a little while when God gave Moses the good news.

Moses picked 12 men, 1 from each Israelite tribe, and sent them to spy out the land.

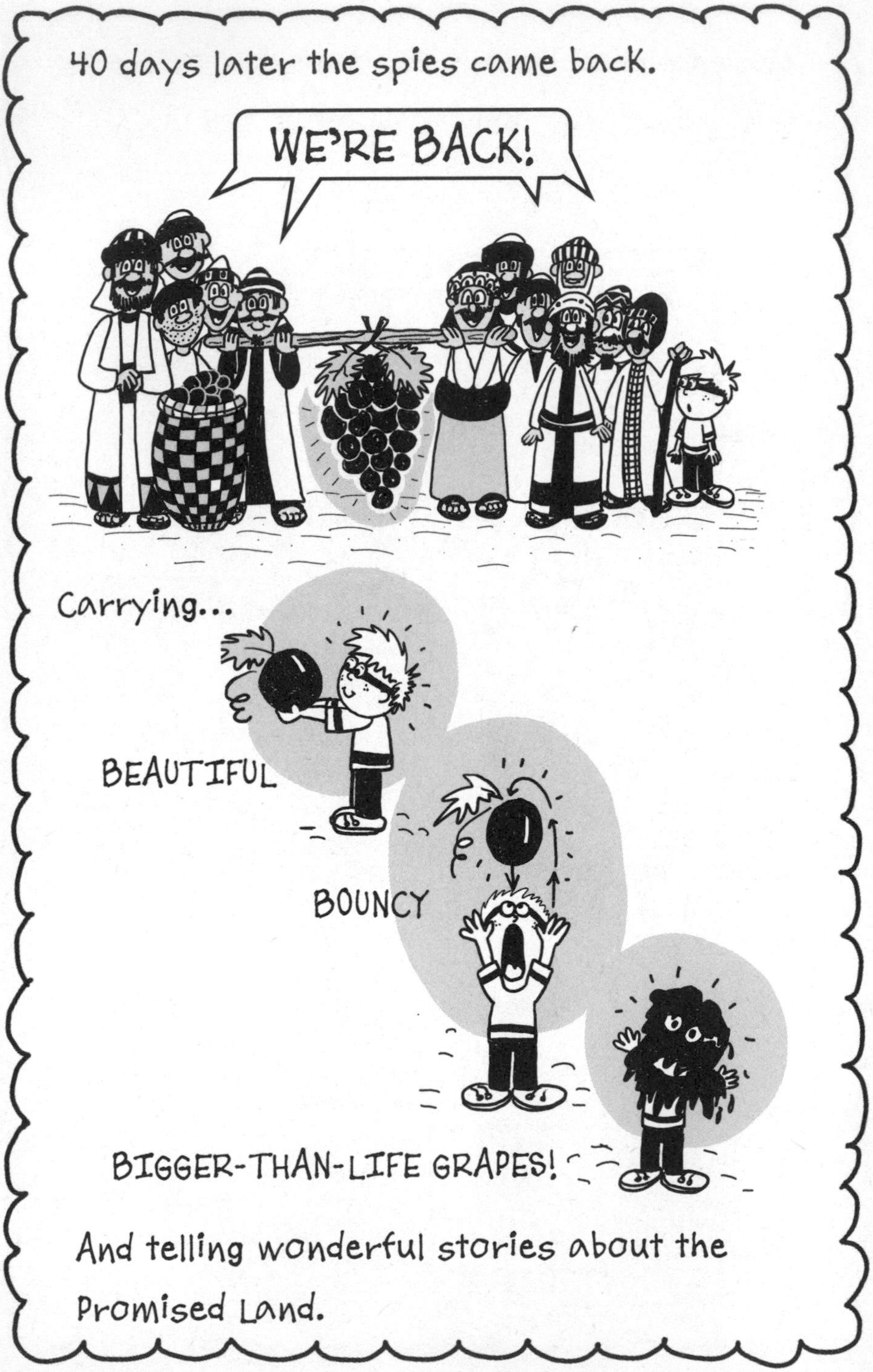
40 days later the spies came back.
WE'RE BACK!
Carrying...
BEAUTIFUL
BOUNCY
BIGGER-THAN-LIFE GRAPES!
And telling wonderful stories about the Promised Land.

But 10 of the spies ALSO told SCARY stories about GIANTS and warned everyone not to go into the land.

The 2 remaining spies, Caleb and Joshua, stuck with their story.

When Caleb and Joshua heard that the FOOLISH Israelites wanted to follow the advice of the 10 spies, they lost it and tore their clothes.

Sure enough, they were right. God told
Moses the **BAD** NEWS!

My job was to draw cartoons on the consequence posters. I found a black crayon in my right pants pocket.

Just in case you're wondering if the 10 spies got a heavier consequence...

THEY GOT TO GO FIRST.

HERE LIES

10 COWARDLY

SPIES

WHO WISHED

THEY'D TOLD

THE ISRAELITES

TO GO

INTO

THE

PROMISED LAND

See Numbers 13:1–14:38

SUNDAY...

Summer's FINALLY here. We're off to visit another grandparent, Grandma McAllister (Mom's mom), in Sacramento.

MOM, WE WILL BE THERE SOMETIME AFTER DINNER!

OK, I'LL SEE YOU FOR DINNER.

It's a total bummer that there's no direct route from Gasket to Sacramento. The longest trip on the windiest roads known to man always makes me sick.

Sure, we can put a man on the moon, but why not invent something really useful... like a car with wings.

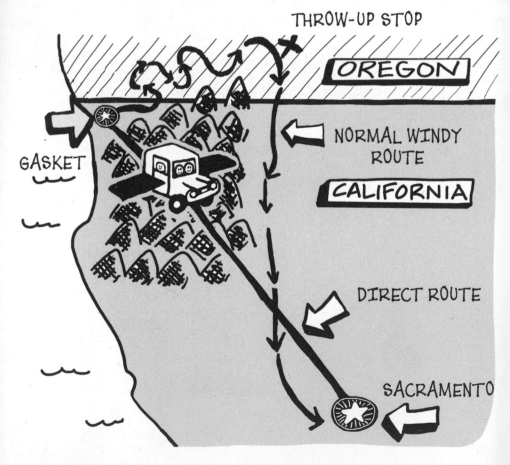

To pass the time, I've tracked our last 10 trips. We average 6 hrs and 34 minutes, door to door, depending on the deer, bear, and moose traffic.

Usually, our drives are one constant argument over what movie to watch. But not this trip.

I was too busy staring out the window remembering my Bible adventure and the non-direct route to the Promised Land. Especially all the ADDED years of walking just because the Israelites chose to listen to the 10 cowardly spies and not obey God by taking their Promised Land.

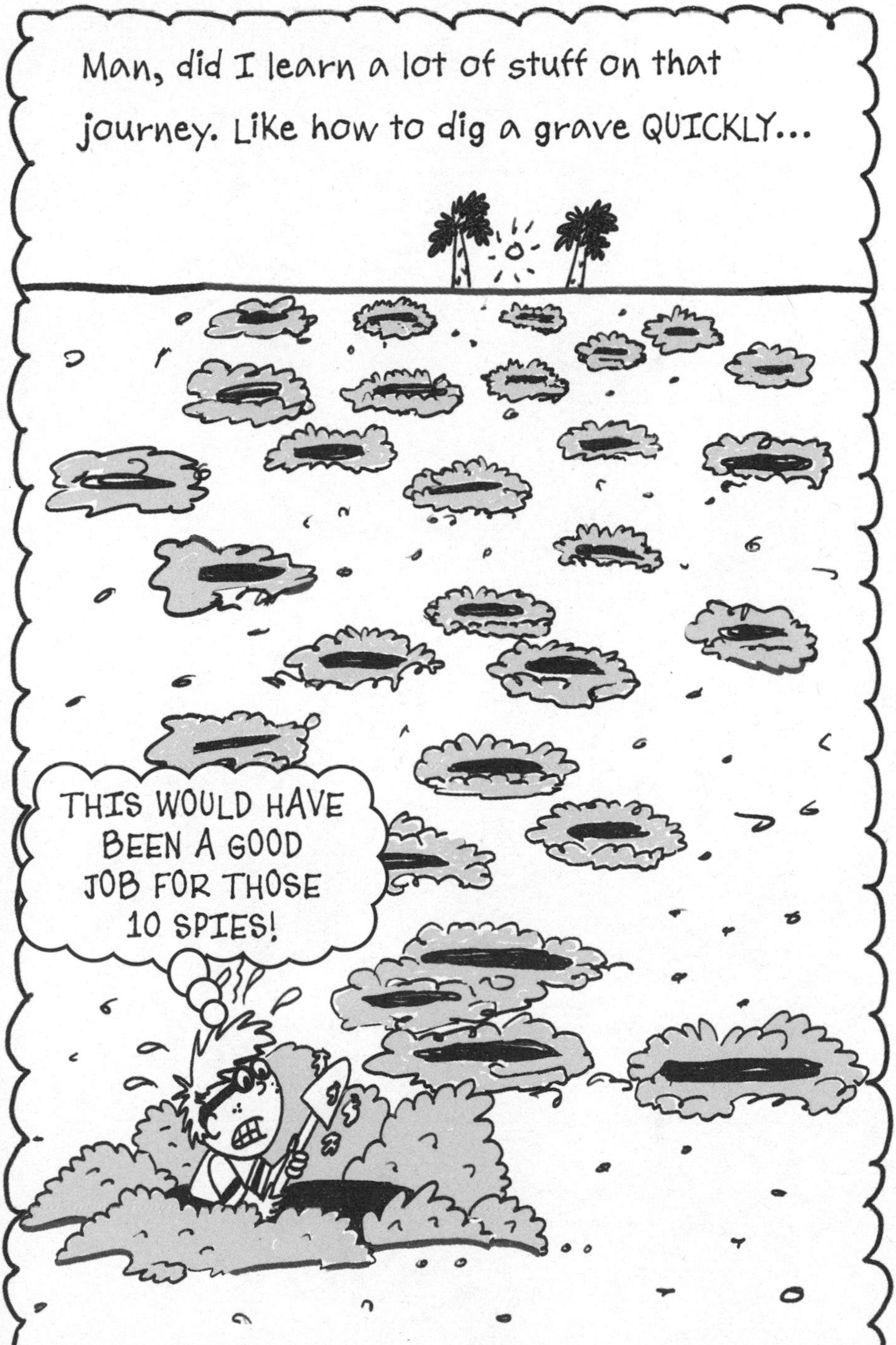
Man, did I learn a lot of stuff on that journey. Like how to dig a grave QUICKLY...
THIS WOULD HAVE BEEN A GOOD JOB FOR THOSE 10 SPIES!

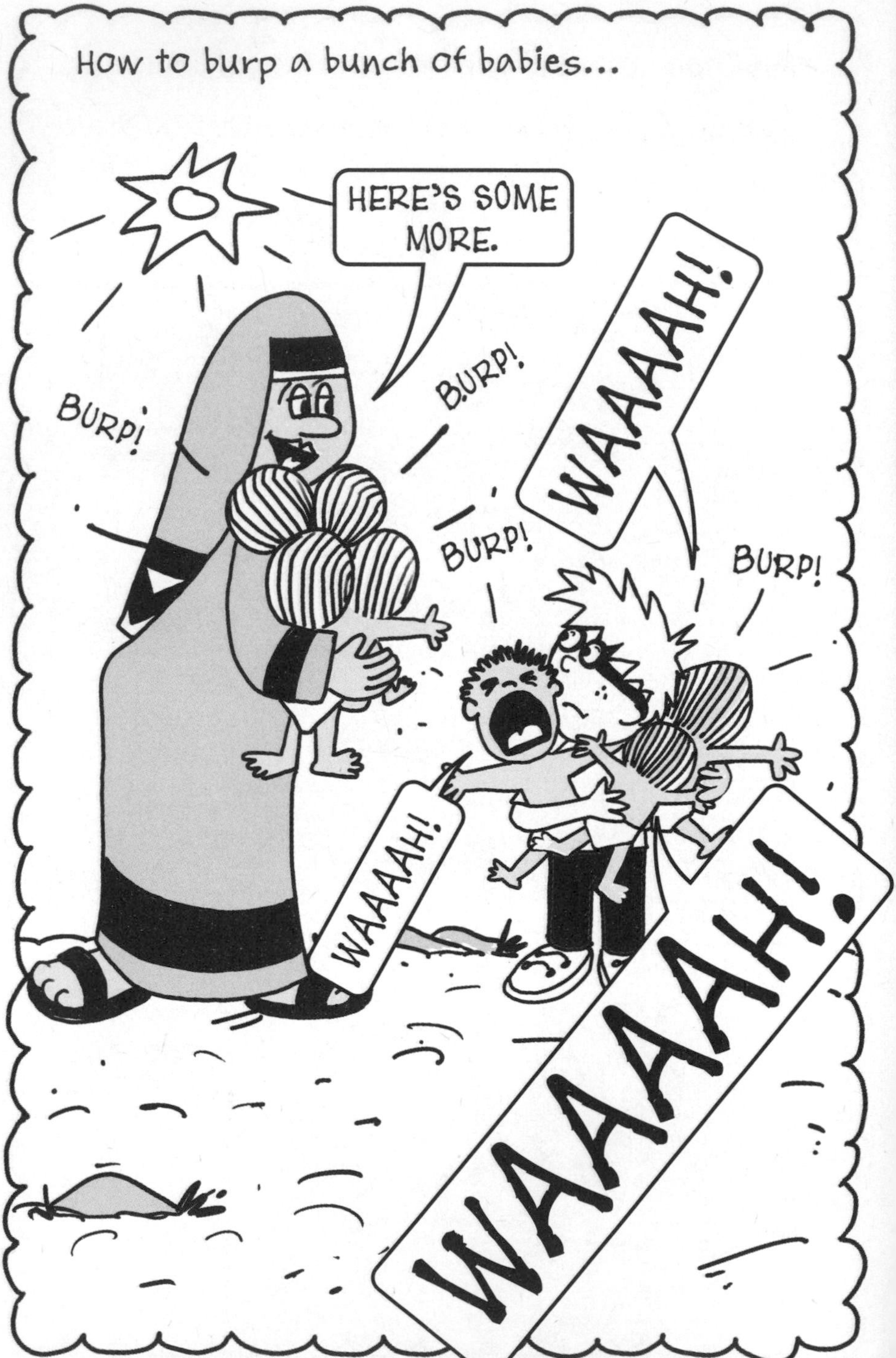
How to burp a bunch of babies...
HERE'S SOME MORE.
BURP!
BURP!
WAAAAH!
BURP!
BURP!
WAAAAH!
WAAAAH!

And how to creatively exercise some toddlers. Which, just saying, got rave reviews from the moms.

IT'S MY VERSION OF A PLAYPEN IN THE SAND.

A PLAYPEN???

WHO CARES WHAT IT'S CALLED? IT WORKS!!

See Numbers 14:26-38

Anyway, thanks to my desert daydream, we arrived at Grandma McAllister's house before I knew it.

Maybe 40 years of wandering is good for something!

SATURDAY...

When I dropped from NUMBERS into DEUTERONOMY, I had another bumpy landing. In my opininon, someone needs to redesign that part of the Bible adventure. Like providing a helmet to keep me from getting a mini-CONCUSSION!

MY RECOMMENDATION TO HEADQUARTERS

BIBLE ADVENTURE HELMET

PATRICK'S HELMET

Moses didn't seem to notice. "Hey, Patrick, can I get your advice? Remember how God raised up a whole new group of people to go into the Promised Land? Well, in DEUTERONOMY, God gave me the job of teaching these people about his blessings."

Since I'm a visual learner, PowerPoint and YouTube are a MUST. Without those options, I was stumped.

Suddenly, out of the blue, I began to envision a MASSIVE sand canvas and me drawing on it. Don't know if it was another mirage or the aftermath of my mini-CONCUSSION.

So I told Moses if he could retell the story of God's blessings REALLY SLOWLY, I would do my best to illustrate.

But it was totally worth it because the result was EPIC. Check out God's live-action drama on the next pages.

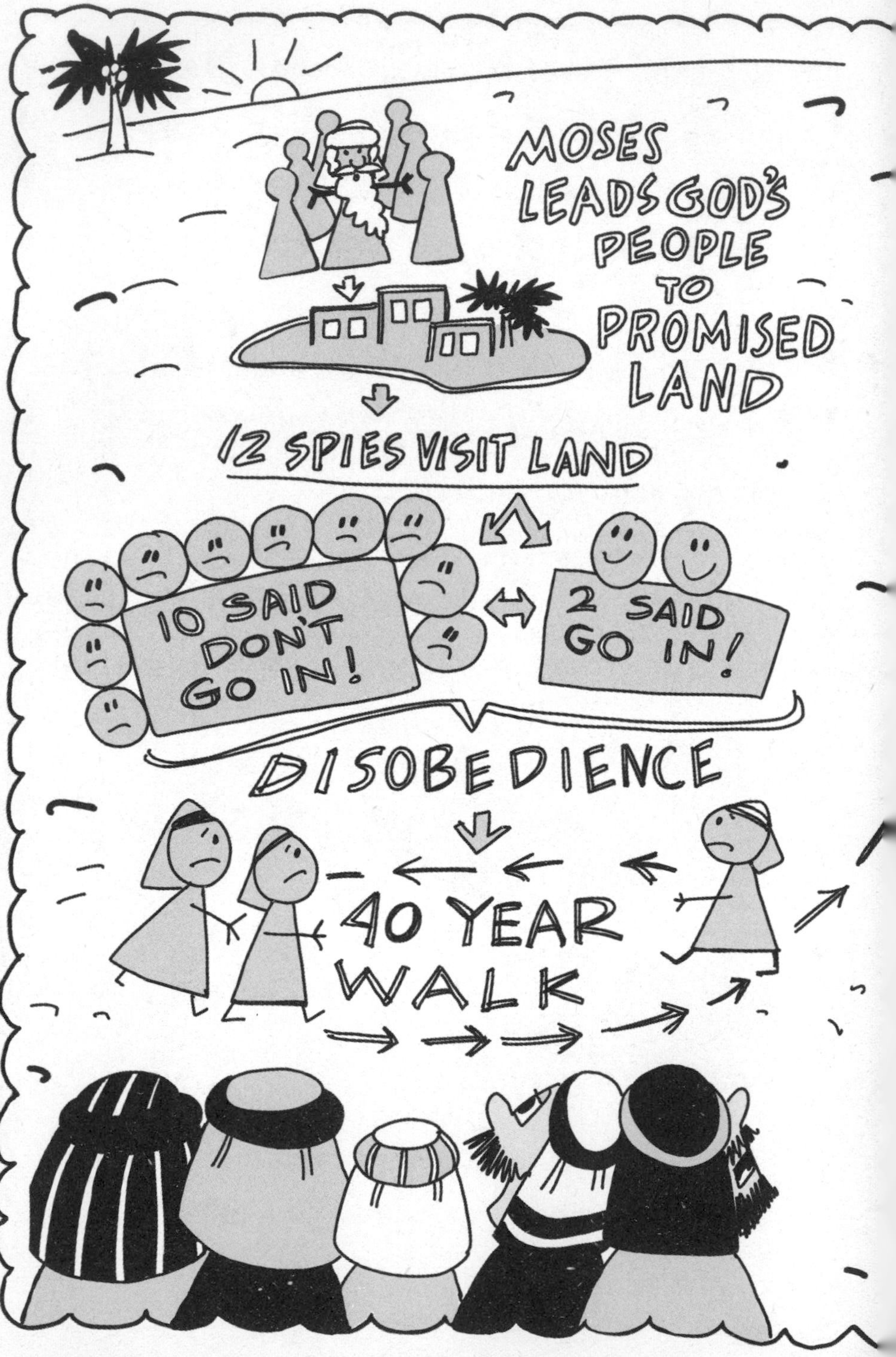
MOSES LEADS GOD'S PEOPLE TO PROMISED LAND
12 SPIES VISIT LAND
10 SAID DON'T GO IN!
2 SAID GO IN!
DISOBEDIENCE
40 YEAR WALK

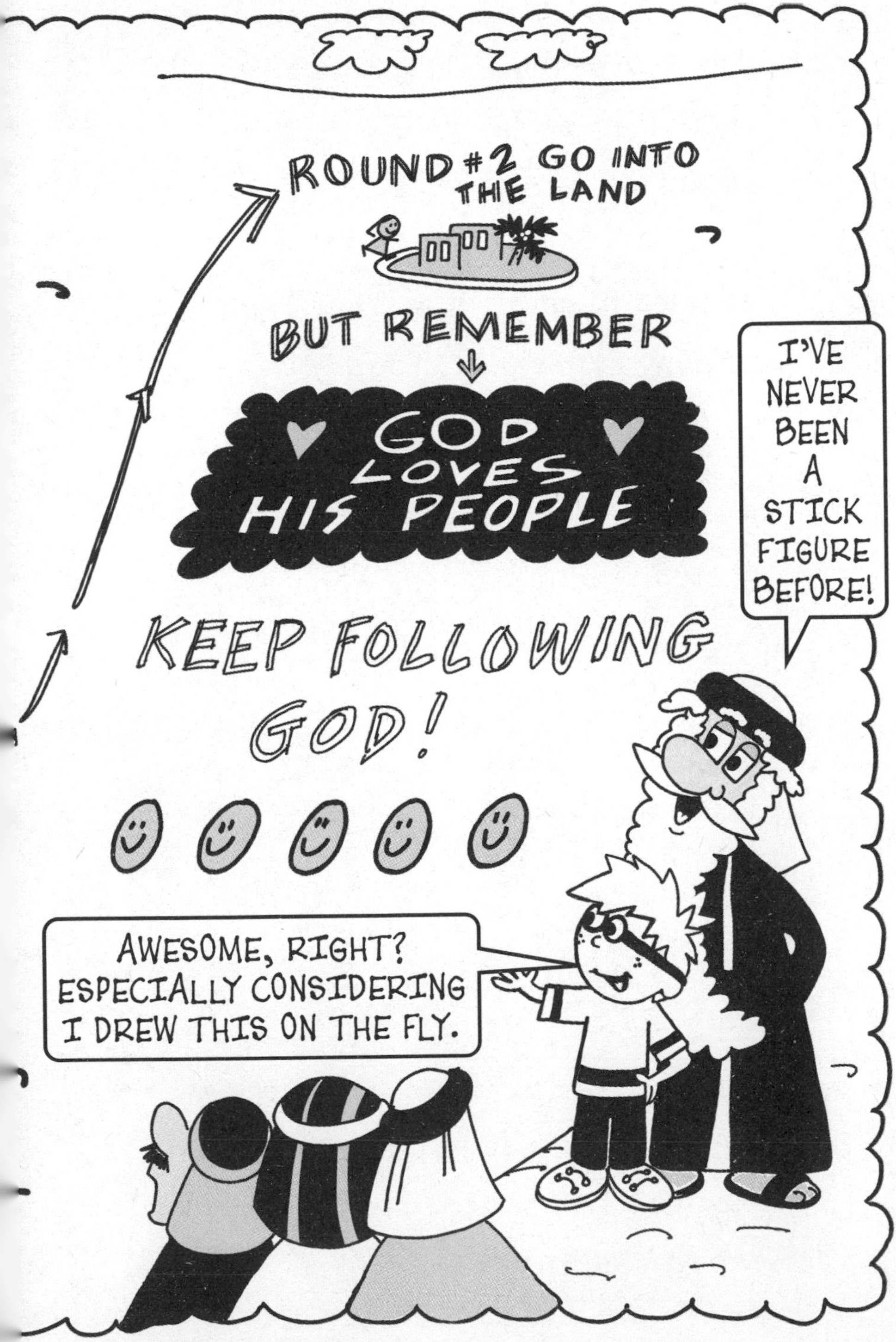
ROUND #2 GO INTO THE LAND
BUT REMEMBER
GOD LOVES HIS PEOPLE
KEEP FOLLOWING GOD!
I'VE NEVER BEEN A STICK FIGURE BEFORE!
AWESOME, RIGHT? ESPECIALLY CONSIDERING I DREW THIS ON THE FLY.

Then the worst thing EVER happened.
A sandstorm blew in and COMPLETELY
destroyed my masterpiece.

Moses tried to comfort me, but I got
stuck in my moment of grief.

It's strange how pain can open up your
eyes. After my sand art pity party,
I looked up at Moses, and all of a sudden
he seemed REALLY old.

Way past retirement age. Somehow I knew that Moses' part of my adventure was about to end.

I CAN'T BELIEVE YOU'RE NOW 120 YEARS OLD.

I KNOW, AND I DON'T FEEL A DAY OVER 90!

See Deuteronomy 1–4

THURSDAY...

Summer is almost OVER. In 2 weeks 5th grade at a NEW school starts.

5th Grade = GOOD!

New School = BAD!

Dad's always saying, "Change is good."
Easy for HIM to say. Every day he works
the SAME JOB in the SAME OFFICE.

While I, on the other hand, am starting a
NEW GRADE at a NEW SCHOOL.

Why change schools, you ask? The new Happy Valley Estates subdivision overpopulated my old school, so they built Horace Gasket Academy (HGA for short).

The one GOOD thing is that Simon and Billy got rezoned too. I think they're the only people I'll know, besides Marlee, who of course doesn't count.

Anyway, Mom's over the moon about HGA's growing reputation.

Today Mrs. Zwingli told her that the school's going to be one of those TOP-NOTCH public schools.

She heard it from Mrs. Stanley, who heard it from the HGA's newly hired janitor. He said they even have funding for a music and arts program.

Then, this afternoon, Dad bumped into
Mr. Newton at the lumberyard.

He found out one more SPECIAL fact about
HGA. Derrick Newton's going there too.

Art program aside, we definitely did NOT
win the school lotto!

SUNDAY...

Graduation Sunday at Good Shepherd
Church today. I love getting certificates.

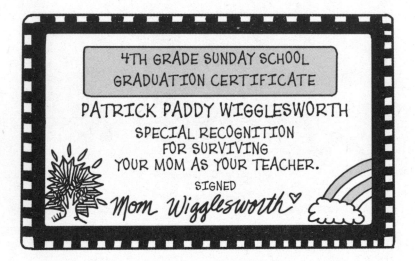

After all, Dad has a wall full of them
hanging in his office.

I figure there's no time like the present to start building MY OWN collection.

A special shout-out to the Dollar Heaven second-chance shop. Their large supply of frame sizes fit my certificates perfectly.

It turns out graduations have been around for a long time. Even the Israelites had a ceremony before heading into their Promised Land. The only lame thing about graduations is they take FOREVER. Especially that one. Moses had to congratulate and shake hands with 3 million Israelites.

ZOPHAR THE CAMEL, "DESERT UNIVERSITY CUM LAUDE!"

The best part of the ceremony was finding a graduation cap in my pocket, decorating it...

and tossing it.

Moses was doing double duty with those handshakes—saying congratulations but also goodbye. God told him he wouldn't be going into the Promised Land, but he could take a sneak peek from the top of MOUNT NEBO.

HEY, A PEEK IS BETTER THAN NOTHING!

I'm not big on long, emotional goodbyes. Way too touchy-feely for me. Fortunately, Moses must have read my mind. Either that or his hand hurt from the jillion Israelite handshakes, because he kept our goodbye short and sweet.

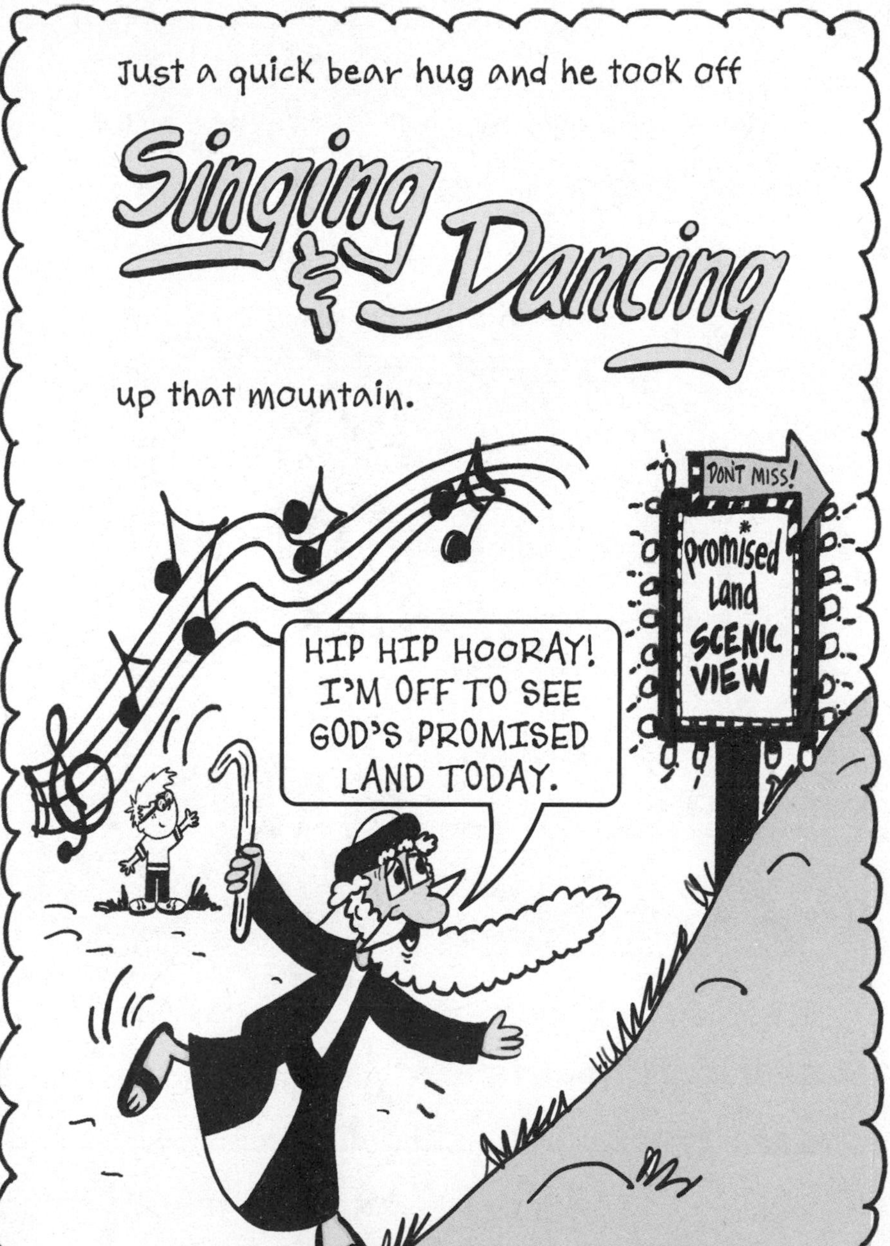
Just a quick bear hug and he took off
Singing & Dancing
up that mountain.
DON'T MISS!
Promised Land SCENIC VIEW
HIP HIP HOORAY! I'M OFF TO SEE GOD'S PROMISED LAND TODAY.
See Deuteronomy 32:48–34:8

MONDAY...

I love sleeping in my tree fort when Mom
lets me. But even that couldn't prevent
a dark cloud from hanging over my head
when I woke up this morning.

School starts today at 8:22, or was that
8:33? WHATEVER! IT'S STARTING! And just
when I thought things couldn't get any
worse, I remembered what Mom told me
last night. HGA is right by Mr. Newton's
work, so of course, Mr. Newton and Mom
buddied up to carpool.

He's taking us to school. She's picking up.

Mom must have sensed how I was feeling,

because she said,

Hmm, SPECIAL RANK, REALLY? Fortunately,
I do my best thinking while brushing my teeth.

WELL, PATRICK, MAYBE A MAN OF SPECIAL RANK SIMPLY MEANS YOU'RE SPECIAL!

SQUIRT

AFTER ALL, GOD ZAPPED YOU INTO A BIBLE ADVENTURE.

BRUSH

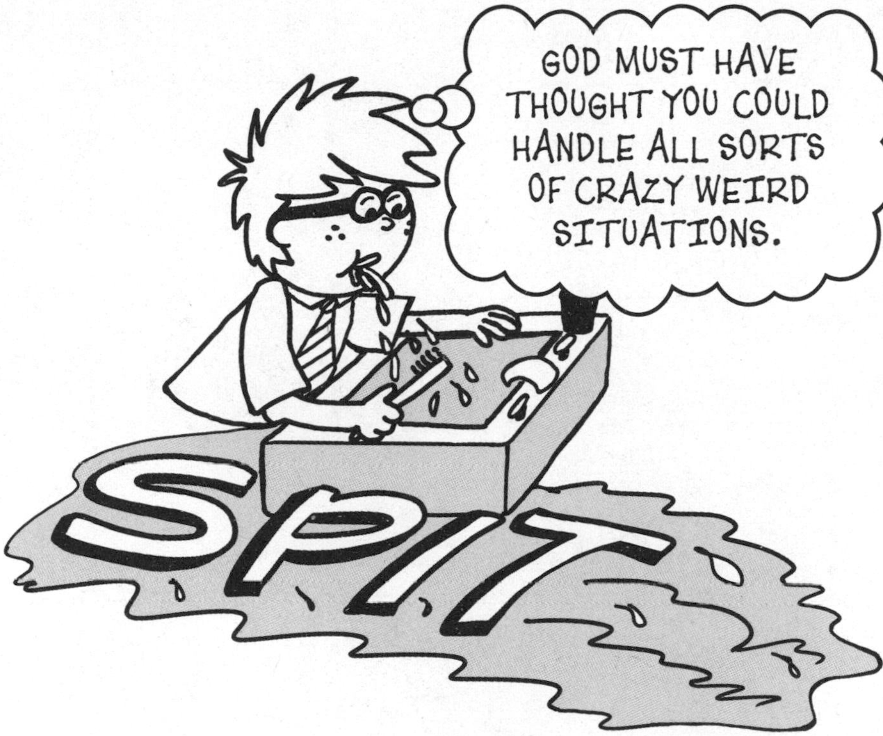
GOD MUST HAVE THOUGHT YOU COULD HANDLE ALL SORTS OF CRAZY WEIRD SITUATIONS.
SPIT

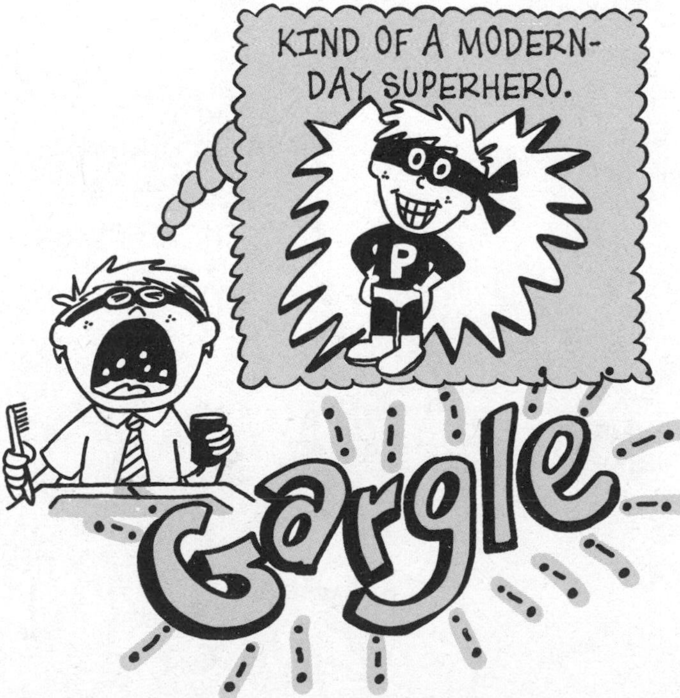
KIND OF A MODERN-DAY SUPERHERO.
P
Gargle

FEARLESS AND BRAVE,

TIRELESS,

AND POSITIVE.

And then, as I admired my sparkling teeth in the mirror, I had one final thought...

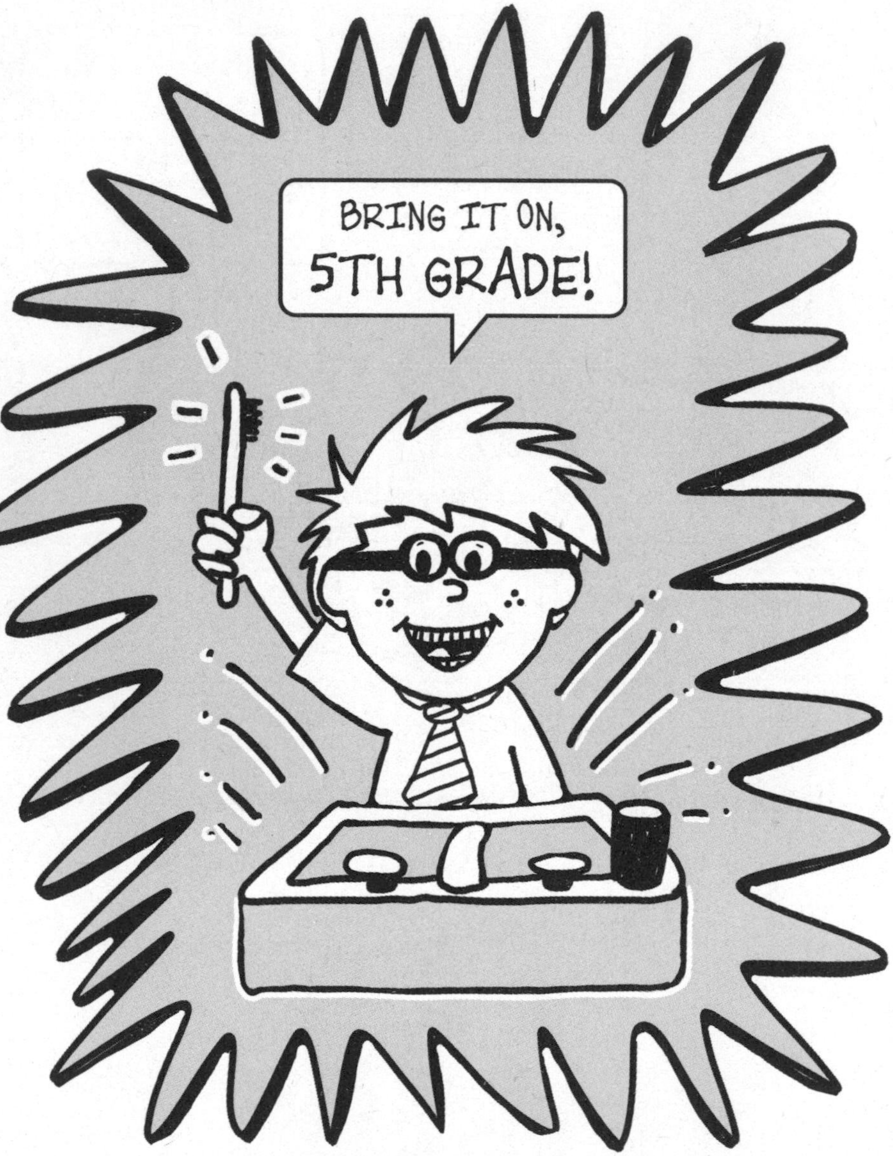
BRING IT ON,
5TH GRADE!

About the Authors

Liz Hagler is the illustrator of *The Bible Animal Storybook* (Questar Publishing, 1990) and *The Early Reader's Bible* (1991). She has a BA in art and English from the University of California at Davis. She studied graphic design at California College of Arts and Crafts and has taught many years of Sunday school as well as homeschooling her children. Liz loves to create images that encourage people to laugh at life and to drink in great gobs of God's grace. Writing and illustrating this Bible adventure book has been Liz's dream for the last thirty years.

Jack Hagler has loved to write and communicate since he was little. Over the years he has been able to use those skills in a variety of venues as a pastor, teacher, executive coach, engineer, homeschool principal, and children's book author. While studying for his MDiv at Western Seminary, Jack's first class was a survey of the Old Testament. It was as if God's plan for the whole Bible was opened up to him. Since then it has been his passion to help kids discover God's goodness and plan for their lives in every book of the Bible. And to top it all off, he gets to do that with his wife of thirty-eight years, Liz.

Jack and Liz live in Salinas, CA, and have three children, two sons-in-law, and three grandchildren. Their first book was *Hooked on the Book: Patrick's Adventures through the Books of the Bible* (2012).